# A SENSUAL LORD

DAVID DAMANT

The Oleander Press
16 Orchard Street
Cambridge
CB1 1JT

www.oleanderpress.com

© 2018 D. C. Damant

The right of David Damant to be identified as the author of this work has been asserted in accordance with the Copyright, Designs and Patents Act 1988.

Cover design by Ayshea Carter
Typeset by neorelix
Editorial oversight: D. C. Damant

All rights reserved.

No part of this publication may be reproduced, stored in a retrieval system, or transmitted, in any form or by any means without the prior permission in writing of the publisher, nor be otherwise circulated in any form of binding or cover other than in which it is published and without a similar condition including this condition being imposed on the subsequent purchaser.

A CIP catalogue record for the book is available from the British Library.
ISBN: 9781999900441

# CONTENTS

# PROLOGUE

I am writing these memoirs in the library of the House of Lords, not as a clerk but as a member of their Lordships' House. Not that one sees many lords here in the library, as on the whole the British aristocracy is built on Character, not Intellect. Maybe my own attachment to intellect, as well my expertise in the arts of love, enabled me to rise from a decent obscurity to my present eminence, if I may so call it. No doubt some of my inherent abilities and the training I had received contributed to my advance up the social ladder in the England of Queen Victoria, although chance as in all human activities, has played its role. I have to confess also that it was as a result of chance that so many of the men and women to whom I have been joined in sexual congress were from the higher ranks of society..... Indeed, including, in England, a Duke and his grandmother the Duchess, and a Grand Duchess at the Russian Imperial Court at St Petersburg.

✶

# A VILLAGE

I was born Edmund Lackland in a small village in the middle of England. It was not so much a village which contained a Big House, but a Big House which had a village, a small hamlet, nestling at its gates. His lordship, the Marquess, ran the county with his fellow landowners. Everything revolved around them – agriculture, the local regiment, the magistrates and local justice..... everything. On any day the house and its courtyards were full of men and women arranging the affairs of the estate and the county, and eating the many lunches provided for them. Yet, even when looking back with the experience of many years and of many political structures, I can see that it was a settled life in which many could feel fulfilled and which could be enjoyed even by those on the lower ranks on the social scale, except possibly for the labourers on the land, for whom uncertainty of employment was added to hard work.

My father was the Second Gardener to the estate, but that was a misnomer, since he was the man responsible for trees – those in the park, and those covering the vast estate over which his lordship ruled. It is important, when looking after trees, to have a steady character and unruffled judgement. A broken tree, or a rotten branch, can kill or injure you or a fellow workman unless you know what you are doing. My father had the steadiest eyes I have ever witnessed, calm and brown, and if I have inherited his qualities of character they have contributed very largely to my life and my success.

My mother was the cook at the Rectory. I have heard that it was the policy of the Church of England, from the Eighteenth Century onwards, to have a gentleman and a scholar in every parish. Our Rector, the Reverend Arnold Bomborough, was certainly both. He had been at Christ Church Oxford, and it was said that he obtained a first class degree. His parish was small, even adding the staff of the Big House, so that he was enabled to write his books on Greek tragedy, which he produced on a regular basis over the years, although looking back I am surprised that there was very much new to say on a topic so well studied in this country and in the relentless academic machine in Germany. He was at the same time a conscientious man, rather severe in manner, but outgoing in temperament. In those days there was no compulsory education of any kind – so that, as Thomas Gray wrote in his Elegy in a Country Churchyard, the talent of an unlettered Milton and so much other talent was lost. But Mr Bomborough introduced a Dame School into the village, presided over by a comfortable dame of mature years, to start the village children off in life. In addition, he and his curates watched to see evidence of native talent in boys (the girls were not in the picture, as far as I could see, but that is the tradition of the age) who were then taught more advanced topics by the curates, or by the Rector himself.

There were in my time three of us pushed forward in this way. With the Rector I got on especially well and one tremendous advantage to me was his love of mathematics – apparently at least in those days men going into holy orders first studied mathematics; I suppose because it was seen as a training in exact thinking. In any case through his tuition I gained a good level of mathematical ability, to which I had anyway a natural bent, and a clear ability to engage a logical approach, which is one reason why I now sit in Parliament as a Peer of the Realm. In addition his wife taught me the basics (and a bit more) of French, which also turned out to be a building block in my career.

The Rector's wife was The Honourable Mrs Bomborough, being the daughter of a peer in the West Country. To say that she was keen on food would be an understatement – she revelled in the pleasures of the table, and my mother and she made a tremendous team. My mother always said that Mrs Bomborough was a better cook than she was, though one must expect such a sentiment expressed about one's employer. I think that the procedure was usually that they would conceive and prepare dishes together, and that my mother with the kitchen maids and parlour maids would act to bring them forward at the appropriate times, whilst Mrs Bomborough, together with her husband, presided in the dining room. And as you can imagine, in the country, with so much fresh produce available, and his lordship's extensive kitchen garden open to her, Mrs Bomborough was able to start with the most splendid materials. She also had his lordship's gamekeepers well trained.

The dining room was magnificent. The Rectory had been built at the beginning of the century for "a gentleman and scholar" to reside there, and the rooms were of classical proportions. I suspect that the room Mrs Bomborough used as the dining room would have been used as the drawing room by her predecessors, and no doubt in due course by her successors. Anyway, it was large – and so splendid was the setting, and so wonderful the cooking, that the Bomboroughs could entertain the most glittering people of the county very regularly, including his lordship on a number of occasions. It was quite a show, and all Mrs Bomborough's aristocratic instincts were brought into play. I wondered why Mr Bomborough had not risen in the church. Only years later did I discover that he had been offered a bishopric, and refused it.

Into this theatre of gastronomy, Mrs Bomborough engaged me to wait at table (a junior footman I suppose I could have been called), even when a young boy. She instilled into me a rule that has been the greatest help to me over the years, and not only in dining rooms – "Service should be exact, but it should be invisible." I fulfilled that principle in the Rectory perfectly. Except that, as I should have mentioned, I have a well-proportioned figure and very blond hair. Dressed for the dining room, I added to the attractions of the room, even though I did not wear the lavish uniforms of the footmen at the Big House.

In those years I came to manhood, and to say that I was above average in the lust that rose in me would be another understatement. Nevertheless, through the character inherited from my father, and the sensible discipline of the Rectory household, I was very careful, especially in such a small community, but the risk that I should break out in an unsuitable way was probably only averted when I met Clara. She was a maid in the house of his lordship's steward, and we had met on a few occasions when she came to assist at the Rectory. We had exchanged glances, sometimes very direct and deep, and, well, I had wondered.....

Then late one dark night we met suddenly in a lane in the village. It was like a reunion of two people who already know each other well. There was hardly need for words. We felt pulled together by strong bonds from the first moment we saw each other through the gloom. By happy chance there was a pile of straw behind some adjacent trees, and with a joint decision we went into the darkness. I was intense in my desire but I found her even more eager and, as I can now see, she was more experienced than I was. It was not for her the first time. We fumbled with each other's clothes and she gave a gasp of delight as she fondled me. I had hardly time to caress her body before in our passion I entered her and possessed her, and felt for the first time the warmth that women have provided for men. How wonderful. And how I thrusted and how violently I came.

We waited a minute and she gave a sigh, it seemed to me of happiness and fulfilment. Then she said, “Well if God made anything better than that he kept it to hisself.”

I think she was made for sex and I would not have been surprised if in later life she had gone on the game. But I never found out.

I went home delighted. I was a man at last. But I had scarcely entered my bedroom when the thought struck me: *What if she has a child?*

I was petrified as I stood there. I tried to sleep but always the thought kept coming forward: *What if she has a child?* In the morning I did not look well and Mrs Bomborough, there being several days during which the furniture in the dining room was being changed, told me to have a restful time, to recover from what she imagined to be a slight cold.

Clara and I had arranged to meet on the next day, so eager had we been, and I went to the rendezvous with mixed feelings. Maybe I should claim not to be well, so as to give me a few more days to sort out my emotions. But any such move proved unnecessary. She was in tears, though reasonably in control of herself. She related how Lord Peter, the second son of the Marquess, had, well, not so much seduced her as taken her. And she had submitted – twice. “I cannot see you again,” she repeated several times to me.

I asked whether Lord Peter would continue. She was sure of it.

"And I cannot resist him," she added. "It is his eyes, and he is his lordship's son."

I had heard that Lord Peter had the most beautiful and penetrating blue eyes, though I had seen him only at a distance, and he had often been away travelling. I comforted her as best I could but agreed that we should not meet again at least for some time. It was only as I walked back to the Rectory that I realised that if Clara did have a child I was in the clear. What a relief.

The next morning Mr Bomborough asked me to attend him in his study, where he had a very grand desk, and bookshelves laden with books. After asking if I was better, he indicated that I could not stay in the village for much longer if my talents were to be fulfilled (as he was kind enough to say). He himself had no definite plan but mentioned that Mrs Bomborough could through her relations place me at Sellingham, the great country house of the Duke of Ramfurline, almost a palace, as a junior footman, to serve in their dining rooms. Of course I agreed to this suggestion, as I was confident of my abilities. As a result of Mrs Bomborough's training I was sure that I could reach the standard required of such a great house. After the talk with the Rector I saw Mrs Bomborough who, I judged, although saying that she would be sorry to lose me, gave the impression that she took pleasure in the thought that one of her trainees could be placed in such a distinguished household. As for me, there was the added attraction that in such a large establishment it would be much easier to satisfy my growing impatience for sexual experience, whilst still acting discretely. It was indicated that it would take about a month to arrange my transfer to Sellingham.

I reported all this to my parents, who were delighted, as they also had thought that their son could not find a real career in such a small village, and as it happened my mother had a distant cousin living in retirement not far from Sellingham. Strangely enough, the idea of my joining the staff at the Big House did not occur to anyone, including myself, and I have never quite worked out why.

And during that month my sexual life was raised to an extraordinary level. On fine days even in winter I used to sit on a fallen tree in a field which was very empty of people, except when wheat was being planted, or at harvest time. In the morning of a day without duties I saw striding towards me a young man, striding, that is, as a member of the ruling class. He wore riding boots and white riding pants (now called jodhpurs) and as he approached he saw me, stopped, and then walked directly at me. I felt at once submissive and when I saw his penetrating blue eyes I knew it was Lord Peter. He gestured with his riding crop and ordered "come along" and took me into the next field where there was a barn.

After we had entered he closed the door and put a bar across to lock it. It seemed to me that he that he had done this before. There were bales of hay in the barn, some in piles at waist height. He wasted no time, putting me face down over a pile and roughly pulled my clothes open. I felt him against me and then pushing into me. He was quite careful at first there was little pain and when I felt his whole body against mine I became tremendously excited. Possessed by the younger son of a marquess!! Then he became more violent in his thrusts and I began to moan and gasp. This seemed to excite him as he thrust more and more, and with a grunt he came in me. There was a pause. Then he pulled out. He ordered me to dress and when I turned to face him I saw his face again, lustful, in command, flared nostrils and with an almost cruel expression. I felt dominated. I wanted to serve him.

"You know the oak tree?" he asked.

Who did not? It was the pride of the park and may have been there at the Norman Conquest. It was also not far from the house.

"Be there at midnight on Thursday," he ordered.

I nodded hardly able to speak. But as he walked away I saw him from behind in those tight white jodhpurs. It was the most beautiful sight I had ever seen – at least until I saw that sight with the jodhpurs off. What proportions! What tight curves! I was a lost man.

The following day I was recalled to service as Mrs Bomborough asked me to assist in the installation of the new furniture in the dining room. The existing chairs and other pieces she had inherited from her parents and were in the style of the eighteenth century, elegant and, in the eyes of the nineteenth century, not impressively heavy enough – they were dismissed as "spindly." In fact I preferred the earlier style, but I have to confess that the room when refurnished did have a more substantial and important appearance. Also the chairs were more comfortable.

For that evening Mrs Bomborough had planned a rather grand dinner, making use of the new furniture for the first time. It was the pheasant season, or rather that season had been in existence for some time, but Mrs Bomborough had had the birds hung in his lordship's game larder for quite a number of weeks. In that cold stone building, away from the house, the birds could become high, that is rotten. I was intrigued by this policy..... surely the pheasants would be better fresh? And I had tasted newly shot pheasant in the past, towards the end of the various seasons when there were plenty of birds available. Not especially exciting, I concluded, and I preferred grouse. When I spoke to my mother about this she laughed.

"I will show you," she said, and on the evening she allowed me into the kitchen early to taste the bird, served in sour cream, another procedure that I found difficult to understand – until I tasted the result. It was served with poached celery. It was a dish fit for angels, if they still walked the earth, and I could see that unhung pheasant was not worth the shooting. With one of Mr Bomborough's fine wines, what a sensation.

That evening we were entertaining the Lord Bishop, who arrived in his full kit, in a colour which I believe is called the episcopal purple, purple from top to bottom – even his gaiters were this wonderful colour. I wondered if he had a cook at the Palace capable of providing food like this. He left in a glowing mood, full of bonhomie. The whole evening was proof that somewhere the Methodists had taken a wrong turning.

I had of course spent some time with my parents, as I was soon to leave, and my mother assisted me in choosing what I should pack to take away with me. They also gave me some small gifts to take to Mrs Warburton, my mother's aged cousin who lived near Sellingham. My father rather surprised me by producing some quite nice clothes, which he had collected over the years as a much younger and slimmer man, some of which fitted me quite well, after a few alterations by my mother. And I am glad to report that both my father and my mother lived to a great age, being allowed by his lordship's successor (with whom I was to have such an extraordinary relationship) to remain in the same house even after my father had retired, having found a suitable young man to take over the trees. I noticed that the young man was very handsome, but happily married.

At midnight on the Thursday I was of course under the oak tree and after some minutes Lord Peter came out of a little gate in a wall adjacent to the house. He led me through the gate and across a small courtyard, and then through a door in a tower and up a circular staircase into a very large bedroom, dominated by an enormous bed. The room was well lit by candles, some of which which were of the large size that I had seen before only in churches.

"When you come again," he said, "the two doors will be open. There will be no need for me to come down."

So he was planning other visits. Anyway, I was at his mercy.

He sat down and waved a hand, ordering me to undress. He lit a cigarette, and then spent some minutes looking at my nakedness whilst drawing on his cigarette. I could not help it, my manhood rose. He laughed and looked pleased. And masterful. He was again wearing the tight white jodhpurs and the riding boots. I gave way.

I said, "Please, sir."

He looked gratified, even more masterful, and went behind a screen and came out himself naked. His skin was like cream, luscious. I wished he had kept the boots on. As in the barn, he wasted no time. He flung me on my back on the edge of the bed, pushed my legs back and then pushed into me. He was hanging over my body like a beast of prey, as indeed he was. And his face more than ever full of lust and power, the eyes flashing in the candlelight as he thrusted and thrusted. He came and I let out a kind of moan. Followed by noiseful pantings. As he withdrew he looked down on his prey with great satisfaction. I felt proud. He ordered me to be there again at midnight in two days time. I left him smoking another cigarette.

The next day I was required to serve lunch in the small dining room. A college friend of Mr Bomborough's was staying not far away and came across for lunch. Mr Bomborough also asked his lordship who had been at Oxford, though not at the same time or the same college as the Rector. I was a bit mystified since the friend, Dr Jameson, was referred to as a Student of Christ Church, so I expected a young visitor, and was surprised when a gentleman of the Rector's age arrived. But Mrs Bomborough (who prepared the lunch with my mother but did not attend the meal) explained Christ Church called its senior men "Students." Rather confusing, I thought. I served a sensational series of wines and the three gentlemen discussed each glass in such an animated and lengthy manner that I would have learned a lot had I been able to understand the conversation. Dr Jameson's coachman must have had the most wonderful meal of his life in the little room off the kitchen, sharing the menu with the dining room. None of the wines, but he was given a glass of beer.

The following day Mrs Bomborough had arranged another special dinner, with the menu this time based around fish which had come in. This was somewhat rare in the middle of England but she had a connection on the Norfolk coast and from time to time some kind of express delivery was arranged. She planned a Sole Veronique, the sole cooked very luxuriously in cream and butter (my mother was able to obtain the freshest and most lovely cream and butter) but decorated with – well, correctly with grapes, but in the middle of England some plums were used, I think greengages (probably the best of plums). Plus little twists of pastry. There were quite a number of other courses, and as in the case of the pheasant dinner the evening was extended, although in the country the dinners started and finished earlier than in London.

Dinners at the Rectory were always in what was called the Russian style, one course after another, rather than the traditional English way of putting many dishes on the table at once. Mrs Bomborough said that that was the way she had strongly preferred from her youth onwards, despite the persistence of the English method of service in some households, especially in the country. That evening Mrs Bomborough and my mother had again extended themselves and Mr Bomborough produced several wines, concluding with an ancient Madeira. He had once or twice guided me round his cellar, though the result was that I made notes in my mind for the future, rather than gathering the origins of each wine at the time.

This dinner was attended by his lordship, a long standing arrangement. Usually he brought with him one of his daughters, either Lady Patricia or Lady Helen, his wife having died some years before. It was with a shock, as I looked out of the window in order to observe his descent from the carriage, that I saw that he was accompanied by Lord Peter, with whom I had an appointment at midnight.

After everyone had arrived they came into the dining room and Lord Peter sat on Mrs Bomborough's right, with his lordship on the right of Mr Bomborough. With a degree of the necessary self-control I carried out my duties throughout the dinner, showing only my usual detached manner, and Lord Peter seemed not to notice the service at all, which was usual of course with the gentry at that time. I wondered whether he had recognised me. But when we retired to the drawing room and I served the Madeira Lord Peter, having accepted his first glass in a formal manner, drank the wine straight down and asked for more, and then more. Fortunately we had two bottles, and many of the guests drank other wines, or the cognac. Although the bottles were of some age the wine did not vary between them.

"This wine is magnificent, Mr Bomborough," Lord Peter exclaimed as, I suppose, his excuse for drinking so much. "Tell us about it."

Which the Rector did, referring to the fact that it was a Sercial, normally regarded as a dry wine, but showing great charm and delicacy, until he noticed that the other guests would prefer other topics. I also noticed that his lordship by several glances seemed not to approve of his son's consumption of the wine.

All in all I had the feeling that Lord Peter was demonstrating something – but what? A signal that he recognised me? And eventually the party broke up and the carriage came to carry the two inhabitants of the Big House back home.

At midnight I went past the oak, through the two doors and up the spiral staircase, into the room now ablaze with even more candles than the first time, and with Lord Peter standing astride in the centre of things.

"Aha, boy" he shouted, coming towards me and hitting me playfully in the chest. "I see that you didn't ration the Madeira."

I replied that it was not my Madeira, but he laughed and said that if his father had not been there he would have drunk both bottles dry. He was almost like a friend.

"And now I have a surprise for you" he added, and from behind the screen..... well – it was Clara, naked under a long dressing gown, I suppose one of his. Whether he knew that she and I had been together before I do not know, but in a few days he had very clearly trained her to the desires of his lust, and now he could have a show.

Which he did, first with Clara on her back and me on top, and then after a rest like little dogs. At first I was a bit self-conscious but soon I felt no reserve and we both performed with great energy. He certainly had a beautiful picture of two young people making love, as Clara engaged in the acts with as much enthusiasm as I did. She and I did exchange one knowing glance, very carefully. I wondered how he would take his own pleasure but that was soon made clear when he dismissed her, I suppose because he could have her at any time. Then he undressed also and I saw again that creamy skin and the lovely proportions of his waist and those beautiful tight curves. He then had me on my back and this time we were both in a happy mood. At least I certainly was and he seemed to be.

That night he kept me for his sexual pleasure very late, arranging me in several positions. When he indicated that I should go home he said that he knew I was leaving the village, and what a pity it was that his suitable boy was being taken from him. Little did he know, little did I know, how closely our paths would be entwined in the future, like our bodies that night.

✶

# SELLINGHAM

My journey to Sellingham was not very comfortable, since the arrangements made by Mrs Bomborough were not observed and I travelled very cheaply. I suspect that the carrier pocketed the difference. The house – although I had of course heard of it by repute – seemed vast. The gardens also had a degree of magnificence which made one gasp at first sight..... There was a fountain so powerful that the jet of water reached nearly to the height of the house, which was indeed more like a palace.

Despite the unpleasant mis-arrangements for the journey I arrived at about the expected time, and was met by a footman who conducted me to the room of Mr Cartwright, one of the three under-butlers (there were also Mr Danvers and Mr Scott, with Mr Benson presiding over everyone). Mr Cartwright was the under-butler responsible for the engagement and training of footmen for the dining room. As soon as he saw me his face lit up.

"Oh good," he said.

"Why good, sir?" I asked.

"Well you see, when a member of the family suggests a footman I have no choice but to engage the man, and who knows what he will be like."

I laughed and from that moment we got on well. His bedroom was the one which had a cupboard in the wall behind the bed in which the gold plate was kept for safety, with an enormous steel door. The silver was kept further forward since it was used so often and was anyway enormous in quantity.

Mr Cartwright pointed out that, apart from my duties in the dining room and in the other rooms where food was served, and looking after the family generally, there were other activities in which I could be involved, some sporting. The establishment supported no less than three cricket teams, one for the indoor staff, one for the gardeners and one for those who looked after the ducal land and forests. The last named nearly always won their matches. After covering several other possibilities Mr Cartwright mentioned that there were also first aid classes, if I was interested. I thought why not, and as a result had a number of training sessions, mostly by Mr Cartwright himself. A training which fairly soon would open the most secret of doors for my sexual activities.

Mr Benson the top butler was a magnificent presence, reminding me of a high priest – not that I had ever seen a high priest, but anyway he was more like my idea of a high priest than the Archbishops I later met in the House of Lords. The under-butlers did the work, two on the occasion of each lunch or dinner, dividing the table between them, and supervising the many footmen. But Mr Benson presided always and his eye missed nothing. All the staff revered him.

I discovered later that three men ran the place under the ducal family: Mr Benson in the dining rooms, Mr Quintin the steward who looked after everything else in the house and garden, and Mr Hamilton the factor who ran the estates. They had lunch once a week, together, to discuss anything that came along. I thought that it was a very efficient way of running an operation like this.

We dined most nights, usually with guests and often with an ambassador, or ministers, or other great men from London. In this way the political leaders of the country met all sorts of other powerful men and players in the political and social game, and this again seemed to me an efficient way to run things, in this case the country. Conversations could be informal, or significant views could be exchanged. I learned a lot by observing this show.

The ducal table was of the greatest interest. Often the number of guests was considerable so that usually the table was long. Charles, the Duke at only 25, was the 12th Duke, his father the 11th Duke having been killed in the hunting field when already a widower. Duke Charles sat at at one end of the great table. He was blond, though not as beautifully blond as I was, and he had a somewhat washed out appearance. Being the duke and so young, he followed the most sensible route and always spoke with reserve, which caused everyone to wonder what he was thinking. Nothing enhances authority like silence.

At the other end of the table sat his grandmother, the widow of the 10th Duke, and always referred to as the Duchess as she could hardly be called the dowager since there was no other duchess around, at least for the time being. She had that welcoming and even kind demeanour of someone with great intelligence, but she also had that absolute assurance of her undeniable position in life. She had the steady and well-opened eye of someone whose happy lot it had always been to command and to be obeyed. She scintillated in a huge display of jewels, some of considerable size, especially her emeralds, but without giving the least impression of ostentation. It was said amongst the servants that she was the only person to whom Mr Benson truly deferred. The Duke and she seemed to have a firm understanding, and no doubt he learned a lot from her for when he would be in sole charge.

The company wore tailcoats with white tie except when the dining room was left empty and little private dinners were held, for example in the Duchess's boudoir, when the gentlemen wore black tie and even smoking jackets, and the ladies fewer jewels. Unlike the evenings I would later witness in London and even more so in St Petersburg, the gentlemen only sometimes wore their decorations at dinner. Our uniform as footmen was dark green with black and silver trimmings, which I thought more elegant than the rather gaudy kit used at the Big House at home.

One weekend when we were entertaining the Home Secretary he was placed on the Duchess's right. The 10th Duke her husband had been a powerful political figure and the man now Home Secretary had been one of that Duke's younger colleagues. Their exchanges were animated, though controlled to some extent during dinner so as to bring the other guests at that end of the table into the exchanges of views and comments.

After dinner they withdrew to the Amber Drawing Room, so called as it contained four great panels of carved amber, the gift of the Emperor of Russia to the 10th Duke when he was our Ambassador in St Petersburg. I noticed, when I was serving the company there with their coffee and some sweetmeats, that the Duchess and the Home Secretary spent a considerable time in conversation. They seemed to be concerned with present political questions on which he was taking the Duchess's advice. I would expect that her experience of such things, as well as her intelligence, would be of great value to him. As they left the drawing room she smiled on me to a degree I thought rather more than I might expect.

After this I was usually placed to assist the under -butler at the Duchess's end of the table. And, after some further days, Mr Cartwright expressed his satisfaction with me, and said that he would write to Mrs Bomborough to say so. The fact that he had also spoken of me within the household became apparent very shortly.

After a few days, and on a day when I was not engaged until dinner, I walked early in the morning to the nearby village where my mother's elderly cousin Mrs Warburton lived in retirement. She had been housekeeper in a house in Sussex.

On arrival in her village I took a wrong turning and, looking up one of the rather confusing arrangements of streets, I saw a man – even from his back his sexuality resonated from him. He was short but obviously enormously strong, and with shoulders so broad that he appeared square in build. The sight hit me so strongly that my legs gave way and I had to sit down on a nearby wall. At this point a local woman came along and I explained (also as a kind of explanation as to why I was sitting down) that I was looking for Mrs Warburton but had rather lost the way.

"O that's fine, luv," she replied. "Just go down the street here and turn left and you'll see her cottage by the big tree."

I thanked her and – the street being the one in which I had seen the man – walked down to see if I could find him again. No luck.

Mrs Warburton's cottage was beautifully kept, with a well ordered garden, and she herself was a very pleasant and outgoing old lady. Having been a housekeeper she was like all housekeepers referred to as "Mrs", though she had as far as one could ascertain never been married. She was a tremendous admirer of our noble families, and had many momentos of the aristocrats she had served in one way or another. I gave her the small gifts I had brought from my parents, and was there when the local Rector called. I could see that they got on well, so that she was not too lonely. He asked about Sellingham, which was obviously a matter of pride in the surrounding countryside.

Walking home by the more direct route I came upon the village smithy. And there, wielding some heavy and red hot metal, was the man. He saw me. He looked up at the church clock which was opposite, jerked his head so as to say "follow me", and closed the smithy for "lunch."

We hardly spoke. He smelt of sweat but in his case I found it provoking, not that I needed any encouragement as he seized my body. I was of course putty in his hands. He had me face up on the bed but held himself above me on his arms as he took me (a good plan as he would have crushed me had he laid on top). And when he was inside me I felt spitted, skewered..... He made many thrusts before he came. I do not know if he liked women as well as men, but he would certainly satisfy them if he did.

I had the thought that I might visit Mrs Warburton rather more often than I had previously planned. Which led my parents, when they heard later about my visits, to believe that I was very kind to their old relation. And, in any case, I grew rather fond of the old lady. Little did she know the other reason why I looked forward to the visits.

In the meantime I was able to experience all the aspects of one of the great houses of England. There was in the park at Sellingham a great conservatory or greenhouse, a very large structure, heated throughout the year and in which were grown the most exotic fruits, including pineapples. The gardeners in the greenhouse were proud of their work and exceptionally proud of their produce. They were exacting in the way in which they produced fruit for the ducal table. They would in the case of breakfast pick the fruits, maybe pears or plums, at the first light of dawn, and by then placing the fruit under glass in the sunlight ensured that it was warmed into perfect juicy condition for the family table. From time to time the Duchess would visit the greenhouse, with her maid, and often with a footman in case anything should be required. I was chosen, and then chosen again. The Duchess had usually chosen also a sunny day, and the whole atmosphere in the warmth and in the glittering sunlight, and with the Duchess beautifully bejewelled, and the exotic trees and fruits, was like a foretaste of Heaven. And I began to realise that in some way Her Grace liked me.

Then one night at Sellingham we had a visitor, Monsieur de Grenoux, from France. M. de Grenoux was writing a book about English graveyards. Why a Frenchman should be writing such a book, and who would be keen to read it when completed, I do not know. But this was his fourth year of visiting us. In the first year Madame de Grenoux also came, but as she spoke no English, and was definitely not interested in graveyards whether English or French, she did not come again. M. de Grenoux spoke some English – presumably enough to discuss graveyards with the locals – but anyway he was usually put on the right of the Duchess if there were no special guests, since the Duchess was fluent in the French language.

On the second night of his visit, as I was standing to the left of the Duchess, I suddenly saw M. de Grenoux's face flush a livid colour and a choking noise came from his open mouth. This was one of the medical problems that Mr Cartwright's lessons had taught me to resolve. I ran round the table, grasped him in the recommended way, at the same time lifting him out of his chair and applying pressure in the right places. He was a plump little man and quite heavy but when, as in the next stage of my treatment I bent him over, whatever had caused the choking fell out. I checked carefully that there was nothing else to fear, and he began to pant in a very healthy way.

Mr Scott who was at our end of the table called two footmen to come forward (there were always a few ornamenting the walls, though for what purpose on other nights I do not know, as they never assisted at the table). They escorted M. de Grenoux to his room, taking for him on Mr Scott's suggestion carafes of water and brandy.

In rushing round the table to help M. de Grenoux I had of course abandoned my usual elegant detachment – and even more so when I was handling him roughly and powerfully as was required for the treatment. As I straightened up I caught the Duchess's expression, held for a brief moment. It was desire. Then the aristocratic mask descended and she gave a short word to Mr Scott to ensure that the atmosphere at the table should return to normal. Since two of the other footmen (of the waiting kind) had stood around me during my cure of M. de Grenoux, most of the table did not realise what had happened.

Well. Well. After dinner I considered. I was certain that I was not wrong. Out of the depths of her personality sexual desire had showed itself in her face as she looked at me, not, as usually, to observe me as a moving statue, but as an active and masculine man. And maybe there was a reason why she had smiled on me in such a positive manner at the time of the visit of the Home Secretary, and chosen me for the walks in the greenhouse. Looking back I am surprised that I did not hesitate more before coming to my decision to have her that night – or rather, in view of our social positions, for her to have me.

As the Duchess retired at a fairly fixed time each evening I had my timing in place. I wore only three things. Rubber slippers (silent). Trousers. And a white shirt. I went up to her apartment by a back stairs route hardly used after the cleaning of the rooms during the morning. At the door of her bedroom I have to confess to a slight hesitation – but what could I lose? I might be fired. Well, never mind.

By the greatest good luck there was in the bedroom an extensive fireplace, and in the grate a large fire still full of embers glowing a bright red. The room was lit by this light and I had a clear line of action. Had the room been in complete darkness there could have been no gradual approach. I walked firmly over and stood by the fire so that the Duchess if she was awake would see me. I then realised that she probably had a bell by the side of the bed to ring in emergencies. I watched carefully to see if there were hand movements to indicate that. What in fact happened was that she moved in the bed. Then she moved again, rising very slightly. She could not fail to have seen me. I walked right up to the bed and stood there for moments. She moved again, I thought possibly in anticipation. So I abandoned caution and pulled out the bedclothes – then she knew it was for real – no negatives so far. I took off the slippers, the trousers and finally the shirt. Then I entered naked into her bed and when even after that move there was still no negative reaction I knew that she wanted me. There was a bit of confused linen in the form of a nightdress but having pushed that away I rose over her, supported on my arms and not touching her body. And she had moved her legs apart!..... I had only to lower my waist to enter her.

I have heard it said that age does not alter what "lyeth below the girdle" and that night I had proof. I was welcomed by a clinging and firm softness. I let myself go, just taking a woman. It did not take many thrusts before I came. And then – the most beautiful sound – she gave a little gasp. I wondered if she had had an orgasm, and how long it had been since she had had a man in her bed. As for myself, as Dr Johnson said, were it not for the imagination a man would as well go with chambermaid as with a duchess. I withdrew and hung over her for a moment. Then I left the bed and went to stand again in front of the glowing fire, this time naked and turning a little for her to observe me. After a minute or two I picked up my clothes and dressed and left.

I went down the back stairs rather as though the stairs were made of air. I had by my action closed the vast social gap between a duchess and the son of a gardener. I could not sleep. I went out into the park (not really allowed at night) and walked and walked, and in the morning hours just washed and dressed. I did not see her until dinner, when all was normal. M. de Grenoux was there having recovered, though he had not visited graveyards that day, but rested.

M. de Grenoux was, of course, very anxious to thank me for my "first aid" and asked me to accompany him on his next visit to some graveyards in pursuit of his research project. I cannot say that this idea filled me with great enthusiasm but he was realistic enough to say that it would only be for one day out of the many during his stay with us. Therefore with the permission of Mr Cartwright I went with M. de Grenoux on one of his tours and found it very much more interesting than I had expected. So much of the history not only of the individual villages but also of the county and even in some cases of the nation were recorded in the gravestones which surrounded our churches. This was particularly the case of course when we saw the graves of the various squires and aristocrats, many of which had played some part in the life of the country whether at the local or national level. And the dates on the graves even of humble people demonstrated the continuity of English life as the centuries evolved. Nevertheless I was pleased that M. de Grenoux had asked me to accompany him only on one day, as the tempo of the visits was rather slow, particularly in travelling between one village and the next.

I was not in any way sure how to follow up my visit to the Duchess, but on my return from my tour of the graveyards I was brought a note, sealed in its envelope, asking me to fulfil a small task in serving a visitor she had invited for a lunch. I told the footman who had brought the note that he could inform Her Grace that I would be there as commanded. What I did not tell the footman was that also in the envelope was a page taken from a calendar with just a few days ticked. I kept the calendar but also memorised the days.

So far, and apart from my liaison with the Duchess, I had not taken any steps to see what might otherwise be available in the house for my sexual activities. Indeed I felt so complete as a result of that liaison that I did not feel the need to seek other sexual outlets very energetically. Also, I had been there only a short time, and needed to find out the lie of the land first. There did not seem to be any gossip amongst the footmen about sex with men, and only banter about sex with women. The sleeping arrangements for the men and the women in the house were, as was always the case, very much separated, though that would not prevent male sexual activity, if there was any. Probably Mr Benson and Mr Quinton kept a sharp eye on that sort of thing.

Then there was another development, which might have turned out badly for me. One of our visitors (I was told that she was a regular visitor) was a Countess, whose husband the Earl stayed in their country house in Shropshire whilst she lived in London with occasional trips to other houses. One could see pretty clearly what her lifestyle consisted of. She liked men and was not discreet about it. She was some sort of a relation of the family since, otherwise, I should think she would have been frosted off. It was rumoured amongst the footmen that she had a fairly regular affair with one of the grooms. Although that was certainly possible, given her very frank personality, I found only one small piece of real evidence. One of the maids I knew told me that when she was visiting the Countess's maid she saw on the dressing table a curry comb, which she explained was the comb used to groom horses. However that may be, it was unfortunate that the Countess's eye fell on me. I say unfortunate since any such liaison could hardly be secret enough not to reach the ears of the Duchess, and then, well.....

On this the latest of her visits the Countess had taken a house in the park, which was reserved for visitors and friends, and for that house she needed a footman. Yes, Mr Cartwright informed me that I had been chosen. I could usually see into Mr Cartwright's thoughts (never Mr Benson's) and I am sure he did not guess at the hidden plan which I am also sure she was putting in place. I was extremely worried, as I would find it difficult to find a credible excuse not to be her footman. Actually, she and I in London later had some of the happiest and most voluptuous times that I had in the bedrooms of my life, as I will relate as my life evolves. At the time I faced a dilemma.

At this crucial moment I was saved by Mr Bomborough's mathematics. The factor, Mr Hamilton, was of the opinion that the arithmetical and accounting ability of the staff in his office needed improving.

Mr Cartwright remembered that, in her original recommendation, Mrs Bombrough had praised (probably over-praised) my mathematical ability. I was therefore transferred to Mr Hamilton's office and as I was no longer a footman of the waiting kind I was not available to the Countess. I wonder if she found anyone else, that is of the kind of footman she was hoping for.

I entered the factor's office rather carefully as I was a new boy and I thought it possible that the others who had been there for some time might resent the newcomer, especially if I was supposed to correct their own work. On the contrary. I was welcomed with open arms. They saw me as someone on whom they could dump the accounting and similar work which they found so tedious. And what I found was that the figure work was very elementary and that it was easy to sort it out.

I say "sort it out" because the financial book keeping and the other records were poorly arranged. The ducal estates and the other financial interests of the family had grown over time, with the relevant documentation usually accurate in itself, but varying from property to property. The record keeping had never been rationalised. I proposed at first to Mr Hamilton a small reorganisation, but his reaction was immediate – "Doesn't the whole thing need re-structuring?" I agreed, as tactfully as I could. And so I began the first of the three projects which transformed me from a clerk to a Peer of the Realm, though I could not of course see the future as I prepared my methodology.

This was to obtain very large sheets of paper and draw diagrams delineating the records of each part of the estate and other properties, showing, in standardised form, the records in each case, and what the relationships were, and where the individual files could be found with more complete details. A good deal of interesting information was thrown up by this methodology – for example, how the balance of wheat as opposed to barley and other crops varied over the different parts of the estate. Of course the people directly involved knew these facts, but to lay it all out enabled the whole picture to be seen by anyone, even for minor and experimental crops. It was also possible to judge more easily the activities of the many tenant farmers. My colleagues were enthusiastic, as soon as they grasped my methodology, with men working late into the evening as each section was built up. In fact this task was in principle not very difficult to do, though the detail was complex, and it was just that detail which my colleagues knew so well, so that they could complete the sections, understanding my overall plan and its consequences. I fitted the accounting into the overall structure. Mr Hamilton was delighted

So delighted, in fact, that he proposed that I should go to the family's London house and carry out the same exercise for the London estates. I confessed to Mr Hamilton my fears about being judged a bit of an intruder in the office there, but he told me that it was the staff in London themselves, on hearing of the changes at Sellingham, who had asked for me to be transferred.

Anyway my work at Sellingham was pretty well done, in its principal structures. My colleagues in Mr Hamilton's office were now elaborating the records without my assistance and in any case I agreed to come down from time to time if required.

I had noted that, on the page from the calendar sent me by the Duchess, that her ticks on the dates suddenly stopped as summer approached. I thought, naturally, that she didn't want to plan too far ahead, as so many things might intervene. And of course on my visits to her bedroom we did not exchange a word. Rather naive of me to wonder why her ticks stopped, since they stopped just at the point that the family would go up to London for the Season, those summer months when the aristocracy and the other landed families joined together in a series of balls and receptions, and young ladies looked for husbands, and young men for suitable wives to produce heirs to their estates. And because of the arrangement made by Mr Hamilton, in due course I went also.

# LONDON

Ramfurline House in London seemed even more vast than Sellingham, though probably that impression stemmed from its setting on Park Lane. I was placed in the family office, and found the records of the London properties in much the same kind of state as I had found them at Sellingham, and susceptible to much the same solutions. Nevertheless, the problems of record keeping were greater than in the country because there were so many individual properties with often different characteristics, and after my initial feeling that the problem was easy I called a halt to myself and proceeded more slowly. Once clear in my mind I ordered the large sheets of paper, and as at Sellingham my colleagues, after initially wondering what I was up to, then cooperated enthusiastically.

The properties in London were of course much smaller in acreage than in the country, but tremendously valuable. The whole plan of the estate was explained to me, and in addition that one of the main activities at the time was the gradual selling of 99-year leases on many houses, raising, of course, very considerable amounts of money, but leaving the estate in place for the next century when the leases would fall in. But there was no clear model agreement and the documentation could easily cause confusion or worse during the life of the leases and at the end.

To take only one aspect of the matter, if the rules on the maintenance of properties near to each other differed when the leases were granted, it would be difficult to keep the street or square in good order externally, not to mention the financial complications that would arise if the balance of expenditure on maintenance varied from case to case as between the estate and the tenants. And many streets and squares were owned as a whole. The individual records were excellent. It was the coherence of the whole thing that was lacking, and having my methods from Sellingham in my mind I knew what to do.

Many London houses of the landed gentry saw little activity outside the Season, but this was not the case with our house. This was partly because the family was heavily involved in politics. One of the Duke's uncles, Lord Michael, was a Conservative member of the House of Commons. As the 10th Duke his father had been a Liberal, there had clearly been a change of party, which seemed to me odd until I remembered that Mr Gladstone had started out as a Conservative – things were rather in flux in those years. Another member of the family, Lord Carleton, was a Liberal member of the House of Lords. So I suppose that both horses were backed. Anyway throughout the winter months and especially when Parliament was sitting many dinners were given by one side or another, so we were not regarded as a house committed to one party – not easy, I would guess, during the great Reform Bill of 1832, but maybe the practice of backing both sides had not begun then.

The staff in the house also seemed enormous, and the atmosphere was different from that in the country. Sexual matters were freely discussed and there was a definite coterie explicitly interested in sex between men. As I was in the family office, I was a little separated from the gossip, though I tried to find out (rather carefully) what avenues of enquiry were available to me. One thing I heard mentioned quite often was "number eleven" but I thought it better not to ask the meaning until I knew who was reliable and who would not gossip about me – not an easy choice to make, as to whom I could rely on. But then by chance I met in the street a former footman who had now moved to another house and although we did not know each other particularly well he at once started to gossip and to talk about "number eleven."

This was, I gathered with some careful questioning, a house at 11 Moreton Square, in which gentlemen could find young men. Apparently they pretty well had to be gentlemen as the cost was high, though the boys got a welcome slice of it. One could go along at the times one chose. Hmmmmm. I wondered what the gentlemen were like.

I was asked on arrival in London to assist in the dining room if they ever had need of an extra hand, though as the place seemed to be always buzzing with servants I could not quite understand why they could ever be short. However my reputation as a waiter had gone before me and I was slotted in from time to time. I think that they found me an asset at the table. And one day who should appear for dinner but the Countess. She recognised me (rather obviously I felt, but no one else seemed to notice her reaction) and she asked the butler to confirm that I had been at Sellingham. He told me afterwards that he had explained to her that the role in the dining room was not my regular role. He seemed to be anxious to probe – none of the grand reticence of Mr Benson. I remained calm.

But in the morning of a free day for me, I met her in the street, whether by accident or by her plan I did not know.

She was very direct – “I am sure that you would like to see my house.”

I would indeed and said so. And by the manner in which her servants reacted to my arrival and to the retreat to her bedroom I would guess that they were used to the visits of her lovers. No doubt her husband the Earl acquiesced in her activities. Perhaps in the country he had a mistress.

I suppose one could say that the Countess was jolly. Her personality was outgoing. As I discovered later, she enjoyed life in everything she did. Leaping onto the bed with her was, one could say, a happy experience. Her movements were voluptuous and varied. When we were entwined it seemed as though we were eight serpents writhing on the bed. The foreplay and the after-play seemed an extension of the times when we were joined. It was a collision of our whole bodies. Time passed and passed. We did well. It was clear that she liked me, and I discovered the virtues of intimate sex with an older woman, the case of the Duchess being so special as to be in a separate category. I had found a regular sexual home in London.

For one event my assistance as a footman in the ducal service was really needed, and that was at a reception and ball given at Ramfurline House by the Duchess herself on the occasion of her birthday. Never had I seen such a dazzling company. As they arrived the guests ascended the great staircase which rose out of the magnificent hall, glittering with gold leaf and lit by myriads of chandeliers, with their light reflected in so many mirrors.

At the head of the staircase they were greeted by the Duchess and I saw, as I stood with my colleagues two to the side of each stair like a handsome guard, so many duchesses, so many tiaras, so many jewels of ravishing size that, until I later attended the receptions in St Petersburg, I felt that nothing could be more astonishingly splendid. As well as what seemed to be the whole aristocracy of England, there were many military men there, often jolly men, but only a few admirals, the others being I supposed at sea or scattered all over our imperial possessions – and the faces of the admirals seemed to include a sense of superiority. Well, I suppose that they did rule the waves. I overheard one of them saying that the Admiralty was concerned about the decline of British naval influence in the North Pacific. Which did not seem to me a very proximate area to be worried about. Still, no doubt they knew best.

My colleagues in the family office were a good deal more experienced and indeed competent than those at Sellingham, so that our progress in restructuring the records for the London estates was rapid, despite there being a lot of detailed work to do. My reputation for sorting out the records and accounts which were involved in managing the properties soon became known in the house and now by the family. The Duke himself called in one day for an examination of what was going forward, and asked one or two very sensible questions. (I appreciate that Dukes always ask questions that appear sensible. After all they are Dukes.)

But there was a significant side effect. Lord Carleton had heard about my progress and also called. He was at that time one of the ministers in the Foreign Office, and as far as I could understand it he was looking after the Foreign Office business in the Lords, the Foreign Secretary being in the Commons. As we went through my proposals he asked many questions, but most of them were about the methodology rather than about how to run the estates. A week later I found out why. He asked for me to be sent round to his room in the House of Lords. I was sent in a carriage – *I can easily get used to this*, I thought. I was expected and was ushered into his room where I found him faced on his desk by three large and, one has to add, rather untidy files. After requiring me to note that the matter of our discussion was a matter of state, and thus not be repeated to anyone not even Charles (he meant the Duke), he revealed his concerns.

The government, he explained, was in the process of negotiating a trade agreement with Russia. It covered many fields, some affecting some of the others, both in agricultural and industrial products, and both governments had been anxious even in its relatively short life to add further items to the coverage of the project which had thus become large. He pointed out that in the Foreign Office (which everyone called simply "the Office,") Russia came within his sphere of responsibility and this business of the Trade Treaty was his to supervise. It was early days, but unfortunate outcomes could be foreseen unless the structure of the negotiations and the Treaty itself were properly planned. Everything had to be coherent.

He and several colleagues in the relevant ministries were progressing the policy aspects of the matter, but he had no one in the Office with the very considerable time needed to devote to the structuring of the various elements of the planning, and preparing the initial protocols of the draft Treaty itself, in line with the policies decided. He had seen at the family office the way in which I had structured the records of the family's interests, to take account of the various complex relationships between the various types of property, the details of the leases, the legal implications and other parameters. Could

I join him to apply a similar methodology to the drafting of the Treaty?

I said yes immediately, of course. But before the idea had sunk in he went further – he added that I would be an assistant private secretary. Now private secretaries in those days were normally gentlemen and for the most part graduates of Oxford or Cambridge. I wondered how I would be received, as someone who was a former footman. Before I could frame a question he answered it, reporting that to work in Parliament and in the Office one needed a certain style and from his own observation and from the comments of my colleagues at Sellingham and in London he could see that I would slot in well. He even added that I had had a glowing reference from the Duchess! Well, she had a rather personal experience of the way in which I handled a very delicate matter.

And so it was arranged. I was given a room in Lord Carleton's house, and found myself now called Lackland, whereas as a footman I had been Edmund. As for the Foreign Office, it was, I was informed, designed by George Gilbert Scott as "a kind of national palace or drawing room of the nation"..... a strange wording, to put the ideas of palace and drawing room together. It was designed to impress visitors and it certainly impressed the young Lackland. I did not entirely leave Ramfurline House, as I went to the family office once a week, but my former colleagues there had grasped the message and could pretty well drive forward on their own, and I could concentrate on the great project of my life, the Russian Treaty. And then I had a letter from Mrs Warburton.

The poor lady had inherited her cottage from her father, and all seemed well for the rest of her life, until, as she reported to me, it was discovered that the thatched roof was about to collapse, and could be restored only at considerable cost. She wrote that she did not want to tell my parents about this, especially as she knew that they were not well off, but could I help? Why she thought that I on the contrary was well off I do not know – or rather, perhaps I do know. It may have been because of my style which Lord Carleton has also noticed. How was I to raise the money?

I had checked in the family office and Moreton Square was not one of the family's possessions. It was in a sort of semi-fashionable part of the West End of London and, as I discovered, really only known to society because there was in one corner a rather large church and larger graveyard. Many funerals, even fashionable ones, were held there. I decided to call at No. 11 and went one day, or rather night when I was free to do so, and I also guessed, as it turned out correctly, that many of the gentlemen would go there only in the dark. Having rung the bell the door opened at once and as I stepped in closed at once behind me. I suppose that it was a procedure to protect the gentlemen clients from being too obviously observed standing outside. There would not be anyone around to observe them at night in that part of London, or anyway no one who mattered, but the gentlemen would no doubt prefer to take every precaution.

The interior of No.11 was rather dark, until I was ushered into the room of Mr Longdon, who ran the establishment. He looked at me with delight – I had grown to be more attractive as I matured, as the Countess had already told me. One could see by his face that he was for a brief moment unsure whether I was a client (my style again, I suppose) or a potential boy, but I settled that by asking how I might make money.

He explained that each boy (that was the term, though we were all young men) had a room with a large couch and a basin. The doors to the rooms had peep holes, so that the clients could check and choose their boys. Quite efficient. As I was flexible and could take either the active or the passive role Mr Longdon was even more pleased. As for the price, which was divided between the boy and the house, it depended on how long the client stayed, the time being usually inside an hour, and he mentioned a fee for me rather higher than the one mentioned to me in the street by the footman. Obviously I would be good bait. But if I waited for a client and no one chose me I would get nothing. As it happened it was a quiet night for No. 11 and rather than try my luck straight away I left and walked back to Lord Carleton's house, calculating how many visits I should need to send Mrs Warburton enough money for her roof. Anyway, I wrote to her next day saying that I would be able to raise the money, though it would arrive at various dates.

When entering into my task on the Russian Treaty, I met in the course of the next few days and weeks the men who with their colleagues in government effectively ran the country – the politicians and the permanent officials. Initially I met those in the Foreign Office and then in other ministries. For the first time in my life I was surrounded by men of the highest calibre, both intellectually and in their character. I felt that the Empire was in good hands. I soon realised however why Lord Carleton had recruited me. The senior men were tremendously interested in the policy aspects of the Treaty and expected the detail to be worked out for them. The junior people, the clerks, on whom the work on the detail descended, tended to be to an extent pedantic, and not to link the detail to the wider picture. This gap I could fill.

And almost at once I was able to enhance my reputation with Lord Carleton and establish a reputation with the wider circle. I found that a memorandum from the Home Office had been carelessly written and interpreted by the Foreign Office in a sense contrary to the Home Office's intention. The Home Office had used figures which included imports and exports when calculating the current surpluses or deficits which existed in a number of agricultural commodities, whereas the Foreign Office had understood the figures to refer to home production and consumption only. Easy to sort out at this early stage but, had the misunderstanding continued, one part of the Treaty would have been a muddle. After I had corrected this people began to ask my opinion on other drafts, and now saw me as a valuable colleague. Lord Carleton was extremely pleased about this since, as I can now understand, he had taken something of a risk of employing me in the first place.

There then occurred one of those events which displayed the impact of chance and fortune in life. Lord Peter's elder brother was killed in the hunting field. Why these aristocrats take the risks of hunting so dangerously, jumping high fences and so on, I can only guess. I suppose it might be that it seems to them something of a release from their usual life of very correct behaviour. Certainly those who did not behave were shunned by the county. As the brother although married had daughters only Lord Peter became the heir, and since his lordship was now somewhat aged I could expect Lord Peter to arrive in the Lords as the Marquess of Martinlake fairly soon.

And, in anticipation of that, as the heir, he had the right to sit on the steps of the throne in the House of Lords, to observe debates, and I saw him enter very soon after I received the news of his elevation. Moving quickly, I caught him on his way out, just behind the throne. He was amazed to see me, as he knew nothing of my career except that I had gone to Sellingham. When I had explained, he punched me gently on the chest, rather like a friend. He revealed, speaking very quietly, that apart from the family house in Berkeley Square he had a secret address in London for other activities. We both smiled at this, in a delighted way. He wrote the address on a small piece of paper and we parted in high expectation of some serious fun. After he had left I looked at the address – No.27 Moreton Square. Well.

Provoked by what seemed a curious coincidence I called at No.11 that night. On the way I walked past

No.27, then in darkness. At No.11 it was clear that the place was crowded: Mr Longdon had a rather cunning way of dealing with a high level of demand – he used interlocking dark corridors and rooms in parallel to prevent one client from meeting another. He grasped me as soon as I arrived and put me into a room, saying "hurry" (we had to undress and wear a kind of semi-transparent dressing gown). Apparently he had a client who was very young and I was needed as the boy who might attract the gentleman. The peep hole clicked a few times and obviously I passed the inspection since the client came in. It was the Duke. Duke Charles.

How I would have reacted a few years earlier I do not know. But in my new and more elevated position in life I felt more confident and indeed, after a momentary pause of surprise I took the masterful line. I had guessed that he would be submissive and that certainly proved to be the case. I ordered him in an insinuating voice to be naked and assisted by almost tearing the clothes from his body. I looked at him naked. Not a bad object for my lust – I had seldom felt more eager. And as for him his eyes widened and he gave a little gasp, almost a cry of anticipation. When I threw him on the couch he pulled his legs back ready and (with some initial care) I plunged into him. He continued to gasp and pant and was clearly desperate for it. When I thrust more violently he became even noisier.

I found out afterwards that Mr Longdon had had most of the rooms sealed for sound, but at that moment with the Duke I did not care. At last having held back a little I came and glared down at my prey. He was in a kind of swoon. His eyes seemed to have no pupils. I then saw that he had prominent nipples and I had the strongest urge to hurt him. There were provided for us little adjustable metal clamps for inflicting pain on nipples if they were prominent enough, and I used them on both his at once, going straight for the highest level of pain infliction. Now his mouth fell open and he made a kind of croaking scream as he felt the pain. I looked down and saw that he was in full erection. I put my hand down and pulled the skin down and tight. He came, with a jet of sperm up to his chin. I felt powerful and fulfilled.

He did not look at me as he dressed. I guessed that he had not recognised me but, even if he had he behaved sensibly, ignoring the recognition. And after he had left I had to sit down and rest as the moral complications of this brief liaison had left me bewildered. When Mr Longdon came in he was smiling so broadly that I knew that the Duke and gone far as regards extra cash handed over. Mr Longdon gave me some of it but I guess he took the lion's share. Well, he had to keep the whole house going. I wondered who had financed it. He had no idea who the client was, and of course I did not tell him. I felt that in some way I should make some sort of a momento of bedding both a Duke and his Duchess grandmother, but could not think of anything appropriate at the time. Some time later I acquired a little toy coronet, with the ducal strawberry leaves, and I bought another to make the pair. But I did not tell anyone why.

A few days later Lord Carleton called me in. He was completely out of his usually calm and indeed happy temperament. He had been approached by the Russian Ambassador on a personal matter, and even the Foreign Secretary was not informed. The Ambassador I had met twice. He was a prince and a very grand Russian aristocrat, one of the descendants of Rurik, the founder of the dynasty that ruled Russia from 862 until, after Ivan the Terrible, the family rather broke up and the Romanovs took over. He had a young and sparkling wife. It was with some difficulty in speaking that Lord Carleton eventually felt able tell me what was the problem.

The Ambassador suspected from the slightest clues that his wife was having an affair, and an affair with someone in or connected with the House of Lords. Could Lord Carleton advise, as a member of the Lords, and as the responsible minister for Russia? He had told His Excellency that he would see what could be discovered, and that I would be informed (though only me), as I might know of rumours and so on. I replied that looking for a lover amongst our noble colleagues opened a wide field of possibilities. Was there no other clue? Yes, replied Lord Carleton, but only one – in some way Moreton Square came into the matter. He had checked that square and no member of the Lords had a house there, though several peers were buried in the churchyard. I kept my face on, with difficulty. I said that I would revolve the matter in my mind.

Lord Peter and I had agreed to see one another at No.27 a few days after our meeting behind the throne, and I called as arranged. He was clearly in a happy and excited mood and I should also have been happy to leap into bed with him and play lovely games, particularly as our relationship had subtly changed, but another matter had to be raised. I said straight out that the Russian Ambassador suspected that his wife was having an affair. He sat down at once and so did I.

"Why am I suspected?" he asked.

I replied that he was not suspected – yet – but that there was one clue. Moreton Square was involved.

"What do you advise?" he asked, rather pleading with me.

I noted that he did not ask why I knew of the suspected affair. I suppose that finding me in an established organisation within the Palace of Westminster gave him the impression that I was likely to be informed of many things.

"Break it off as quickly as you can" I replied. "Just do that."

And I was able to help him to see the matter in perspective by telling him that no one – even the Ambassador – knew anything about him and his name was not involved. So far. I knew that he was the man because I knew of his address in the square. No one else did. But if it got out it would cause an international incident, and he would be shunned by society and ostracised by Her Majesty.

He stood up and looked out of the window. "I will break it off when I see her tomorrow," he said. "But she is a wonderful person, as well as being wonderful in bed."

"Perhaps I can find you another woman like that, but without diplomatic complications," I replied, thinking of the Countess.

We exchanged a few more words and as I left I could see a determined look on his face and hoped all would be well.

And when two days later we met by arrangement, he told be that all was indeed well, as far as he could see. She had burst into tears, related that there was no one she loved except her husband, and that she would never be tempted by such foolishness again. Lord Peter was naturally relieved and we actually embraced as though we were French or Italian, and agreed to meet after a week or so – after which time I would have unravelled the matter in the way I would, but which I did not of course tell him about.

As soon as possible I arranged to see Lord Carleton, and when I entered his office he saw at once by my body language that I had some news.

"Well, have you found out anything?"

"The matter is resolved, sir. The liaison has been broken off, with the lady showing remorse at her foolishness, and quite clearly in love with her husband."

"And who was it?"

"You will appreciate, Lord Carleton, that I have to respect confidences on both sides. Such matters can be unravelled only if those concerned can rely on secrecy."

He gazed at me for a moment in some surprise. Then he stood up, walked round his desk and, as I stood up also, he shook my hand.

"You go from strength to strength. I will inform His Excellency at once."

And by these means I was looked upon by the representative of Russia in London in a deep and important way, to my great benefit as the work on the Treaty evolved.

As Lord Peter had acted to a certain if limited degree honourably, I decided to go ahead with my idea of introducing him to the Countess. I was of course in touch with both of them and arranged to call on her at her house, with Lord Peter. I thought it better to conceal his address in Moreton Square. He could reveal that to her in due course if they got on. And they did. They were both of course experienced at taking lovers, but in the case of these two the mutual attraction was so immediate and strong that after just a few minutes of conversation I made my excuses and left. When I saw him next he expressed tremendous gratitude, and said that in return he would tell me about No.11 Moreton Square. He meant, I am sure, to recommend it to me as a client. And before I could say anything he revealed that it was an investment on his part, and a profitable one providing that an eye was kept on the manager. I laughed and said that I had been a boy there, but added untruthfully that that was quite a few years ago. He laughed. His eyes were still beautifully blue.

As a result of all this diplomatic activity, if one could call it that, I had not gathered together very much for Mrs Warburton, so I went late that night to No.11. I had sat in my room for only a short time when Mr Longdon introduced an Indian gentleman. Well, he was rather more than just a gentleman – he was of the Maharajah type, gorgeously dressed, with many jewels adorning his garments, his throat and his hands. Mostly red stones which I had every reason to conclude later were rubies.

When he saw me completely naked he glowed with happiness and was himself naked in a minute, apart from a wonderful ruby collar, and a ruby bracelet on one wrist and another on an ankle. He was dark skinned, of course, and had the most beautiful pattern of dark hair. I suppose he saw my white skin and my blond hair as a contrast which he found delicious. His embrace was warm and comforting, if that makes sense, and he came immediately, and then after a pause came again. He took the active role and I suppose would not care to perform otherwise. After the second time he looked at me and kissed me with, it seemed, affection. So much so that just before he left he turned and gave me a ring with a large red stone. I bowed, not being able to think of any other way to show my deep appreciation. Mr Longdon came in and, as with the Duke, appeared very pleased with the money received from the Maharajah, and gave me what again I suspected was not my agreed share. But I had the ring carefully secreted in my clothes.

It is not easy for a servant to sell jewels. The jeweller would at once suspect that it was stolen property. However, I was able to explain this difficulty to Lord Carleton, mentioning that I had inherited a ring and I thought to sell it if it was worth anything. He at once gave me an introduction to one of his jewellers in the form of a letter, in which he also said, very carefully, that he would be pleased if they gave me a fair price. Dressed most formally, I visited their shop in Bond Street and handed the letter to them. I at once received the most obsequious service, since Lord Carleton's name commanded attention. And the ring – they were astonished. It was indeed a ruby.

They asked (I suppose they had to) where I had obtained the ring. I answered, from my late uncle who had been the business manager for a Maharajah in the neighbourhood of Hyderabad. This seemed to them a very good explanation since, although I had not (they thought tactfully) referred to the Nizam of Hyderabad, they were, of course, aware of the mountains of jewellery that were possessed by that ruler. They gave me a price. I was astonished in my turn. It was enough to send to Mrs Warburton all that she required and leave me with funds which would assist me in my new role as a gentleman, though I remember cautioning myself – *Be careful, Edmund, keep in balance.*

I soon began the significant part of the work on the proposed Treaty. In fact, I threw away everything I had done up to then and started again, having by then really understood the relationships between the different parts of the Treaty. This involved close work with the Russian Embassy, and the people there were amazed at the facilities that the Ambassador made easily and at once available to me. But soon I had them on my side, and a veritable cascade of memorandums flew around London. At first my activities were referred to by the senior people as "Mr Lackland working away" but soon major policy decisions were made and they found how easily and efficiently those decisions fitted in to the preliminary drafts of the Treaty.

Until, that is, we began to be held up by delays and inconsistencies in what we received from St Petersburg. One complication was that the laws in Russia and in our own country were of course different, and might therefore clash, and that was a point that had to be watched very carefully, especially as the laws or, at any rate, the usual procedures were not always coherent with each other even within one country. And the same was even more true of existing treaties, not only those between ourselves and Russia but more problematically those with other countries, which had to be taken into account as the Treaty with Russia was being developed, since when the Treaty was in place these treaties with third parties would, of course, still have to be honoured. And for these and many other complications we needed speedy and accurate cooperation from St Petersburg and we were not getting it.

There was only one way of putting this right, and that was for me to go to St Petersburg and indeed, after discussion, that is what Lord Carleton decided. The Russian Ambassador in London would give my arrival there a very firm push, and I would be on the spot to try to get the procedures on the Russian side sorted out, and coherent with what we were doing in London. Also, in view of the stage reached by the work in London I could rely on the material coming to me in St Petersburg to be timely and accurate. Our Ambassador there would provide every facility.

I recognised that with this arrangement I should really be in charge of the development of the Treaty as a whole, subject only to the policy decisions handed down to me. My only request, in agreeing, was to take with me Weatherhead, one of the clerks in the Office who had been involved with my work and who spoke fluent French. That was the language of diplomacy and I would do my best, but someone more fluent in the language and also familiar with the Treaty would be a great facility. Plus he could assist in improving my French. Lord Carleton agreed and within a month I was travelling to the most amazing and grandest capital in the world.

✶

# ST PETERSBURG

The journey to St Petersburg was long and tedious, made more tedious by the Russian customs. Although I was to join the British Embassy and had very extensive documentation to prove it I was on an ordinary and not a diplomatic passport (Russia was one of the few countries that required passports). They went through everything I had with me. The real difficulty arose in the case of one of my trunks, which contained only a great pile of my large sheets of paper, since I was not prepared to risk not being able to obtain such sheets in Russia. They could not believe that I was not some sort of tradesman. Eventually, however, I got the message and found – Why! Here is some money!! – and all was then well.

On arrival at our Embassy I found that the Ambassador himself was there to greet me. He indicated that apart from some high level discussions on other topics (I suspected, as it turned out wrongly, that there were none,) the Treaty was the main activity in his embassy. I was allotted a small bedroom, an elegant study and a large office in which, by my request in advance, there were several large tables for my sheets of paper. I was given the honorary rank of third secretary, the lowest but still a diplomatic rank, and which attired me in a rather fine military style uniform, green with a red collar and silver epaulettes. Everyone in St Petersburg seemed to be in uniform, even the servants and the streetsweepers in uniforms designed and coloured according to their roles. Our Ambassador was anxious that we should not look *sous habillé*. And I was *de facto* in charge of the drafting of a most important Treaty.

St Petersburg glittered in the snow, as it was the winter, and indeed the Season. Whereas in London the Season is in summer, the opposite is true in Russia. It was cold and everywhere one went the heavy coat, fur hat, gloves and scarf were taken away as one entered a house or palace, by servants who remembered whose coat belonged to whom. No tickets. The shops in the grand boulevards gleamed with luxuries, including jewels of all kinds, and boxes and other treasures fabricated from gold and silver. And as for the Orthodox services, the glamour of the church buildings, the flashing colours of the icons, and the deep deep voices of the priests, gave me an insight into the Russian character. Rich and powerfully romantic. But perhaps this last thought reflected my English temperament.

I was very soon invited to wonderful parties, so lavish as to make the grandest of London parties seem somewhat restrained. These parties were extensive in time, sometimes lasting over several days or even for a week, with people always there, dining or dancing or playing cards, and with the most beautiful flowers from the South of France, and little trees in pots from the Crimea. At dances and other events attended by the Emperor he sat at an imperial table, raised and aloft, commanding the whole scene. The champagne was either rather sweet or very sweet, in the Russian taste, and I soon got to like it. I imagined pouring it over Lord Peter and licking it off. And the other way round.

As for the dinners, the arrangement was, I discovered at once, to start with what the Russians called "small things" or *Zakuska.* Fortunately the French is more understandable – hors d'oeuvres – though that is the usual word in English also. These were served to the guests standing up in an ante-room – caviar in quantity, always very fresh, smoked fish, sour cream, pickled vegetables and many other things set out on long tables. One had to hold back on one's appetite as the doors then opened on the dining room and we sat down for a dinner at which many courses were served – of course *a la Russe* as Mrs Bomborough had related. In between the courses little yellow cigarettes were smoked, filling the room with aromatic haze, through which the jewels on the women and the medals and decorations on the uniforms of the men would flash and gleam. If the Emperor were present a gold service would appear but, as one of the aristocratic ladies said to me, "a gold service looks very well but it allows the food to grow unfortunately cold. I never use mine except when I am entertaining His Imperial Majesty, and as this is the case in most households I doubt if His Imperial Majesty ever has a hot meal."

These invitations were the result of a number of letters of introduction given to me by the Russian Ambassador in London, and the British Ambassador in St Petersburg. And as I was presentable, spoke some French, and was recognised as working on an important Treaty, soon the invitations multiplied and I was on many lists.

In particular, I was invited to two houses. The Grand Duke Paul, one of the eighteen Grand Dukes in Russia, the male descendants of recent Emperors, took me very much into his circle, and I visited so often as to become almost what the French call *un ami du maison.* His wife the Grand Duchess had skin which at a distance, or even close to, looked like marble, though I was soon to find that it was as soft as silk. She was a lady very much poised, though not at all austere or grand, and it was not long before I realised that she had her eye on me. But I remained for a time detached in manner, until I could obtain a better knowledge of society and the Russian people, or at least the Russian political class.

The other house which began to send me pressing invitations was the French Embassy. The embassies had not, as one could understand, been covered by many of the letters of introduction I had received. But as soon as we met at the Grand Duke Paul's, the French Ambassador invited me to call, which I did. He was very elegant both in his dress and in the language of his body movements, and seemingly very much in favour of me. In fact I began to suspect that he had certain ideas for games involving myself. I noted also that there was no ambassadorial wife. My suspicions were proved shortly after the initial visit. This had been in his drawing room, with many servants around. But after I had enjoyed a party which he gave the next day he asked me rather meaningfully whether I would like a late cognac at a date some days hence. I agreed, and he smiled, I think a smile of triumph.

The work on the Treaty in St Petersburg proved to be difficult. The trouble was that that the records, and the letters of communication, had not been kept by the Russians in any rational way, and much of the detail was, to a greater or lesser extent, chaotic. I could see that the only thing to do was to start afresh, not upsetting the existing methods but starting another track in parallel, properly designed, and transferring information to the new track only when appropriate. There was nevertheless one man on the Russian side who was completely on top of the subject – and he was indeed the only one. This was Monsieur Valerian (always using French term). I had the impression that he did not welcome my arrival, but orders from higher up had insisted that he worked with me. And he did, and I have to confess that he was relentless in his efficiency. He also spoke some English which helped and after a bit he had some insight into my method and worked with me in transferring the various independent trade agreements into my system – here, as in my previous projects, drawn out on my very large sheets of paper. When he was with us he and I decided on the readiness of each part of the material. When he was absent, my excellent clerk Weatherhead from London and two Embassy staff who had been assigned to me put the jigsaw together.

But we could never get it perfectly to fit. As we tracked the financial flows (which, of course, were dependent on the volumes of the various exports and imports but my system was set up to deal with that,) there always seemed to be some small sums missing. We just could not sort it out. I was careful that I said nothing to Valerian about this, and neither did I allow my team to do so. These discrepancies would not have been noticed without a system as coherent as mine.

After a day of frustration about this snag, I went to the Grand Duke Paul's and found a special gala in progress. It was a splendid evening, during which I experienced something very odd. The Grand Duke had a dwarf, always around. I think that he found the dwarf a way of relaxing, as he was a kind of clown, a fool in the old sense. The dwarf spoke only some obscure dialect of Russian which only the Grand Duke could understand. I had seen the little man before but on this evening I passed quite close to him and he looked at me with his usual smile, which suddenly and briefly turned to intense lust. Then he reverted to his smile. I wondered what sexual activity such a being would expect with me? I decided to make no move – in fact, to avoid him.

In any case at this point the Grand Duchess came up to me and made it clear that we should dance, which we did (it was a waltz, which was the only dance I could really engage in). At the end of which she sat me down on a glittering couch rather distanced from the throng.

"My husband is very understanding," she said in English.

"I understand also" I replied.

"At one o'clock be at the door in the street on the little canal," she added, and asked me to escort her once more to the dance floor, but as it was a Mazurka I had to decline. I kissed her hand, and we parted. Well..... She had made her point.

If I were to classify the Grand Duchess's style in bed, I would say that she was languorous, indeed excessively so. Our embraces were slow and sophisticated, elegant and sensual, and not violent. We did not tumble about as I did with the Countess. And her skin was the silkiest I have ever felt, so much so that I stroked and stroked, and I could see that she relished my reaction. My thought was, as I came for the second time (no exotic positions for her), that if it were true that her husband was relaxed about this I had a wonderful bedfellow in St Petersburg. Only later did I realise that she must of course have a list of men and probably a long one.

At that point in my time in St Petersburg I received a letter from the Rector in Mrs Warburton's village, a letter both tragic and amazing, brought to me by the Diplomatic Bag. The poor lady had died, but when she had received the funds which I sent to her for the repair of the roof of her cottage she had been so delighted that she left me everything in her will, having no family heirs. And, it transpired, she had at just about that time unexpectedly inherited an estate in Sussex, small but valuable, from her former employer who had left it to her, after the expiry of a life interest, "as a tribute and as thanks for many years of faithful and kind service." What this "service" had involved was explained by the Rector in his embarrassed and therefore unnecessarily long letter. He had discovered that Mrs Warburton had been not only the housekeeper for her noble employer but also his bedfellow for those "many years." Well, I had not expected that. That explained the legacy of the estate. I was now a rich man, or fairly rich but, more importantly, was possessed of a landed estate. I could not help but reflect that the kindness expressed so wonderfully by Mrs Warburton was probably due in part to the impression made by my frequent visits, so that the blacksmith also played his part in my good fortune. As regards the cottage and her other possessions, I asked the Rector to apply them to parish purposes. And I thought it best to report my inheritance in Sussex to Lord Carleton.

On the occasion of the next reception given by the Grand Duke Paul the Grand Duchess was away, but I met the Grand Duke Michael, the very elderly uncle of the Grand Duke Paul. Michael had been at Cambridge and seemed extremely well informed about English life and society. He remembered the 10th Duke of Ramfurline as ambassador, and had later stayed at Sellingham. I reported that his duchess was still presiding there with great style, at which he expressed delight. He then remarked that there had been, at Sellingham, a very bright young footman called Benson, who stood out amongst his colleagues!! I was able to tell him that he had shown skill in spotting the young man as Benson was now the high priest of the house. All in all we had a splendid conversation. I was sorry to learn shortly afterwards that his age had led him to retire from society. It would have been wonderful if he could have visited Sellingham once again, to meet the duchess and Benson. Both would have been delighted to meet this link with the past. But I was able to inform both of them that I had met the Grand Duke Michael, and I was able to pass on his recollections.

As the Grand Duchess was away I left the palace reasonably early. Midnight was striking on the church clocks as I walked through a very dark and cold night and I began to realise that I was being followed. By the dwarf. I am I believe very wide in my tastes but could not imagine what the dwarf and I could do in the bedroom which would please me. However, tolerant as I am, when we reached the Embassy I let him join me as I entered through a side door. When we reached my apartment he avoided the bedroom and went straight into the study, where he pointed to the chair next to my desk, obviously inviting me to sit down. Which I did. And when he knelt between my thighs I realised his intention. I have not, in the course of many sexual encounters, found more than a marginal pleasure in a man's mouth and tongue, or a woman's for that matter, but there was an exception and this was it. I have never felt such intense pleasure. He had an amazing technique. I have never come more violently than I did as he finished his task. He even let go in the most smooth and gentle way. Then he stood up and bowed, and left. Perhaps I could now comprehend – or perhaps only guess – why the Grand Duke was so understanding of his wife's taste for other men. He could achieve his own exquisite satisfaction in another way.

It was strange to work in a capital ruled by an absolute monarch. At first, I could see that the system was different but as everything in England was done in the name of the Queen I assumed a difference only of degree. But I soon began to see that the difference was large and significant. Nor could I feel that it was efficient. The respect which even powerful men in London showed for the Commons and the Lords just did not exist in Russia. There was no parliament, and no democracy, and the reference of everything to one absolute centre of power seemed to me to twist every discussion into a shape which did not and maybe in many cases could not arrive at a balanced conclusion. It did not appear to be a system that could handle change and even more had not the ability to impose change. Well, I suppose our record in Ireland is hardly an example of efficient government but, in Russia, the constraints on good government were pervasive. Nevertheless, in the case of my own work, the initial push given to the project by the Russian ambassador in London, and the continuing support of our ambassador in St Petersburg, ensured that the various ministries were reasonably efficient in their cooperation.

As a result the Treaty was progressing well apart from the small discrepancies, but about those I was deeply worried. My system was coherent – so why these errors, or what seemed to be errors? So the next day I told my three assistants to take the day off. Then I sat down and went through everything – every detail, every link, every entry. Still no enlightenment, until I realised that I was almost late for the French Ambassador's "cognac."

Well, I was ready and, although there was indeed cognac, it was soon followed by a rapid transfer to the bedroom. His Excellency was slim and elegant and had the most delicious moustache, carefully trimmed and with the ends pointed and slightly upturned. Wonderful for kissing, as I found at once. Perhaps I should write a monograph on the use of the moustache in kissing and fellatio, and indeed for many things. I suppose that he was over sixty but still as I soon found very definitely the active partner. He took me, rested a little and then took me again, most energetically. An admirable performance, I thought, for a man of his age. As he went to the next room to wash I saw his body from the back, very tight and youthful. And then since he closed the door I assumed he would be away a few minutes. Sitting on the edge of the bed I saw his grand ambassadorial tail coat lying on the floor where he had thrown it in our passion – I went to pick it up so as to hang it properly..... as I did so a paper fell out of an inside pocket. I should not have read it of course, but I did. It was a bankers draft for a large sum payable to Monsieur Valerian. I put the paper back in the pocket and left the coat on the floor.

He shortly returned and give me another of his stunning kisses. "Now you take me, my darling boy, and then I must sleep. I have an audience of the Emperor early tomorrow."

So I took the active role and looked down on his smiling body. He seemed pleased. I was puzzled.

That night (or early morning) I went to bed and to sleep still puzzled. Within an hour I woke up with an almost physical shock. Valerian was in the pay of the French. The Treaty was his main indeed his only activity. He must be distorting the Treaty in the French interest. Why else should the French pay him? That's why he had resisted the idea of working with me. But in what way could he serve the French?

I leapt at the papers and rethought everything. The small sums that I had noticed were being syphoned off, and once on the track I could find where those sums were going – to bank accounts in three Russian towns, which we had previously thought were trading centres but which, on examination with my new insights, seemed dead ends. Why was the money going there? Of course the sum in each case was small, even tiny, rounding errors in currency exchange transactions for example – amounts not to be noticed unless the control systems were as perfect as those that I proposed – but overall, as the Treaty was implemented over time, the money going to these towns would add up tremendously. I organised my thoughts and made an appointment to see the Ambassador as soon as I could that morning.

I laid out the matter for His Excellency, though dissembling as to how I had seen the bankers draft drawn in favour of Valerian. When I had finished he asked again for the names of the three Russian cities to which money would be channelled. Then he stood up and looked out of the window for some minutes. Then he sat down.

"I will reveal to you, Lackland, a matter of the highest secrecy. Regard it as such. The Russian government has some evidence that a foreign power – which power is involved has not been discovered – has a plan to bribe certain Russian governors in the provinces, on a considerable scale and on a continuing basis. These governors are powerful men, often far from St Petersburg, and with a great deal of latitude in the exercise of power in their provinces. A foreign government able to influence their decisions would be tremendously well placed in so many political or financial or other fields. You will be aware that money talks in Russia. But though those plans have been suspected by the Russian authorities the information is very incomplete. And no information could be obtained as to how such large sums could be transferred into this country on a regular basis without becoming known. I was consulted as it was thought that perhaps London as a financial centre might provide a clue. But I found nothing. We only found that the cash was supposed to come from within Russia, which seemed odd, and in particular from two Russian cities – and these are two of the three cities you have mentioned to me."

"I can only say, Your Excellency, that although one should not be too speedy in linking these two matters, the apparent coherence is persuasive."

"Yes, and it is very persuasive. I will see the Russian Foreign Minister today. Please remain available and please do not see Valerian."

"I will ask the clerks to stand by for the time being and I will put off Valerian with some excuse."

"Good. And hold yourself available."

The Ambassador was at the Russian Foreign Office all that day. On the next morning he came to my office and had me go through the whole matter, looking at my sheets, and taking notes (Ambassadors usually carry such things in their heads). He was again away on the third day and the fourth. That evening I was due to attend a performance of a ballet at the Maryinsky, a performance honoured by the presence of the Emperor. I left a note in the Embassy in case the Ambassador would want me that evening and joined the Grand Duke Paul and the Grand Duchess in their box. I am not, exactly, too excited by the art of ballet, except to lust after the dancers of both sexes, but I had to admit that the standard that evening was exceptional. The corps de ballet were sensational, moving beautifully, and the male and female principals seemed to float in the air. But in the interval, before we had even started on the caviar served in the little room behind the box, a servant entered and whispered something to the Grand Duke, who became agitated.

"The Emperor has asked to see you," he exclaimed, and the servant (actually I think he was an adjutant of some sort) led me to the Imperial Box, where I found a dazzling company.

I was presented to His Imperial Majesty by our Ambassador. The Emperor did not say very much but what he said was enough. He even spoke in English.

"You have served my country well," he said.

Then, taking a box from an aide, he decorated me with a Russian order, with a star of some magnificence and a beautiful silk sash. I bowed, thanked His Imperial Majesty in what I hope were appropriate terms, bowed again and returned to the Grand Duke's box, where I created a sensation. Not only had I been decorated by the Emperor himself in such a public manner, but my decoration was apparently of a high order. Of course no one in the box that evening knew why I been decorated, although the decoration and the reason for it were all over St Petersburg the next day. How this sort of information leaked out I cannot imagine. In any case that evening I was to a degree in a state of shock, which enabled me to sit through the second act of the ballet. I was told afterwards that I ate most of the caviar available, and the servants had to bring new supplies. This amused the Grand Duke and the Grand Duchess, though it was from a semi-conscious nervousness on my part rather than anything else.

The next day the Ambassador went over the matter with me. As was obvious from the Emperor's action, the discovery of the French plot had hit the Russians like a gunshot, and one part of their reaction was to look upon the British Embassy and of course especially me with great approval. The French Ambassador had been informed that he was *persona non grata*, and Valerian just vanished, whether to execution or to Siberia I still do not know. Within days I had a pile of invitations from every house in St Petersburg, so much so that I had to ask the Ambassador to filter out the ones to accept. As was the custom, men wore their orders at many of the receptions and balls, and I wore mine, to the astonishment even of those already aware of the award. It was a miraculous time, though I had my rule – *Edmund, keep in balance.*

And yet, at the same time, it was a society rather too rich and exotic. I began to yearn for the calmer and more intelligent though perhaps less brilliant society in London. And at this point my life was in fact unravelled in an unexpected way. I received a very detailed message from Lord Carleton not only saying that after my absence they needed me in London to finalise the Treaty, but also that I would be entrusted with a special mission to Berlin on the way home. At the same time in order to ensure efficiency at the Russian end they would send Lord Carleton as the Ambassador to Russia, as the present ambassador was, in any case reaching the age of retirement. Weatherhead my excellent clerk would stay on to provide assistance and continuity, much to his delight, though what he was up to in St Petersburg I felt it better not to enquire.

And so it was arranged. The Ambassador lent me his social secretary to write to everyone in St Petersburg, especially and in the correct terms to the Emperor. I myself wrote the the Grand Duke Paul, and indeed I had a final and on this occasion exhausting fling with the Grand Duchess. But I never saw the dwarf again.

# BERLIN

And so I set out for Berlin. I had read a great deal about the establishment of the German Empire under Prussian leadership and I had studied as much as I could about Germany in general as soon as I received the instructions from Lord Carleton. But I was surprised to find Berlin and especially Potsdam still manifesting the military spirit to such an extent. Officers of the German army commanded such respect, in the cafes and on the pavements, and Potsdam was nothing more than a military barracks. The remark by Mirabeau that Prussia was not a country which had an army but an army which had a country seemed still to be true.

As a result of the introductions that I had been sent from London I was able to visit Frederick the Great's palace of Sans Souci. He was indeed possessed of genius and not only in the military sphere. Also I must confess that anyone who builds a palace with the place for dining as the central room has my immediate and high approval. The rooms in which Frederick lived seemed to me to have a somewhat inferior decor, and I learnt later that they had had been redecorated by his nephew and successor, Frederick William II.

My mission in Berlin was with members of the Great General Staff, which in every way controlled the German army. Their position was raised to an almost incredible level of power by the genius and success of Count Moltke, whose reputation and aura affected every conversation, and not only on military matters. It seemed to me that civilian opinion was not given enough weight – I had the feeling that military questions could so easily override broader political aims. One could see that so long as Prince Bismarck was around there was someone in charge to keep a balance, but he would not live for ever. I was sorry not to meet him but he was away at his estate.

I had been entrusted by Lord Carleton (in fact by the Foreign Secretary) to convey a note of official thanks to the Great General Staff for a military study which they had kindly shared with London. This I did in a very formal manner, accompanied by a secretary from our embassy in Berlin. I assume that it was more of a courtesy to send the thanks by a special representative, rather than through our embassy. As a result of my mission I was asked to attend two receptions in Berlin, at one of which the Emperor was present. There were many conversations in English, although my French came in useful.

But I was concerned to observe an apparent dichotomy in the German view of my country. Several of the leading men in Berlin were at one and the same time very friendly towards England and jealous of our empire. It seemed to me a very unbalanced point of view. Germany already held the greatest military tradition in the world and the most magnificent army. Surely she should see herself as a satisfied power? In these conversations I maintained a calm demeanour. But there was an undertow, a desire for Germany to manifest itself outside the European continent, mentioning, as it appeared, parts of Africa which they considered available to them, even amongst people not close to the government or to the General Staff (and those who were close would not of course have touched on these topics to me). I reported this impression to Lord Carleton, together with a very private note that our ambassador seemed perhaps too friendly to the court to which he was accredited.

As I was leaving the second reception I realised that I was being accompanied – that is, followed very closely – by a tall and most handsome young officer, wearing the red stripes on his trousers that indicated that he was a member of the General Staff and therefore a very bright star. I had seen him during the reception and had looked at him several times, since he had the authoritative face and intense blue eyes of Lord Peter – the eyes were paler in colour than Lord Peter's, though equally intense. And his hair was as blond as mine, though cut shorter. As we walked nothing was said until we arrived at the door of our Embassy, where I was staying.

"A pity," he said.

"Why a pity?" I asked.

"You are at your Embassy and I am at my barracks. It will be difficult to meet."

I felt an urge, a tremendous desire, to fight with him on a bed. But there was no possibility.

"When do you leave?" he asked.

"The day after tomorrow," I replied.

"Give me your address..... maybe I will come to London at some time."

I handed him my card, with my name and the details of the Foreign Office. Well, he was a man of high responsibility.

And he did come to London, but years later, when he was a general. We laughed about it, but regretted that nothing had happened on that evening in Berlin.

# LONDON AGAIN

I arrived in my England to find a note from Lord Carleton (not yet *en post*) asking me to call on him in three days, at a time stated to be very crucial. So I had two full days to recover my bearings, and indeed at midnight on the day of arrival I felt so consumed with lust that I went round to No.11. Much to Mr Longdon's surprise, I announced myself as a client not a boy.

But hardly had I arrived when Lord Peter emerged from a side room, having heard my voice. We laughed and punched each other and would have embraced had we been alone – and Mr Longdon was amazed that we knew each other and indeed very well. Rather than stay I, of course, went along to No.27. We drank a bottle of champagne each, over which I discovered – which I did not know – that his father had died and he was now the Marquess of Martinlake. And when I began to talk about Russia he exclaimed, "Oh yes! You are the golden boy.

Lord Carleton reported your achievements in the House yesterday."

I realised that unless I was careful all this would go to my head.

"I had better be brought back to earth," I remarked.

"How?" he asked.

"Take me," I said.

At which he leapt at me and had his way as though we were still in the same relationship as when he first met me in the barn. But in fact by now I rather loved him. We agreed to see each other regularly, and I left and went to bed, fearful only that something might go wrong in my life after such a string of successes.

It was strange being back in London after the glamorous life of St Petersburg. It was in a sense like returning to earth after a visit to another planet. Life seemed so much more realistic and one got the feeling that clear thinking and common sense were the prevalent methods of thought. I do not know how far this was due to the fact that England was a democracy and that matters were discussed in an objective way. Or at least that was what we set out to do, even though differences of opinion and differences of interest muddied the waters in so many ways. In London I felt that I was in the presence of rational organisations and I concluded that if the Russian system was to work efficiently they would need an Emperor of outstanding intellectual and moral qualities. Maybe like Marcus Aurelius, not that I am particularly familiar with the politics of the Roman Empire. And the chances of hereditary monarchs producing heirs with those qualities are pretty small. I suppose Queen Elizabeth is an example of a dynasty producing an outstanding head of government, but this must be rare.

This feeling of being in a different universe was enhanced when Martinlake (as I now called him) took me to one of his clubs, where a quiet decorum reigned. Aristocrats have several clubs and some of them did not allow members to bring guests. This was true of Lord Michael's club the Carlton, from where the Conservative party and when they were in power the Empire was run. It was said that it was easier to get from the Carlton to the House of Commons than from the House of Commons to the Carlton. The company at Martinlake's club was, I could estimate, younger than at many clubs, since he had joined this one as a young man looking for young company.

However one old gentleman was there and spoke not at all until the end of the evening when he turned to me and asked suddenly "How was your wheat last year?" Not having any wheat either last year or ever, I was at a loss to answer, when fortunately Martinlake broke in and reported on the crops on his estate. At this the old gentleman burst into life and an animated conversation ensued, especially on turnips. The company at the club was, I suppose, a microcosm of the ruling class, with most excellent wine, and food suitable for the nursery. Well, one thing the English are not good at is food, Mrs Bomborough and my mother being exceptions. Otherwise, it is not surprising that so many French chefs are employed, and that there are now more French restaurants appearing in London.

I called at Ramfurline House, where my achievements on the Treaty were known, though they had not heard of the Russian order conferred on me by the Emperor. The Duchess received me and had a somewhat reserved manner, as though she knew something which she could not discuss with me. As I realised later, Lord Carleton had informed her of what was in progress for me. I thought also that she was ageing, and for the first time she appeared leaning on a cane. And indeed this was not surprising as she was over 80, and I then realised why the birthday party that I had attended before I ceased to be a footman had been planned on such a scale. She realised that it was her last great party. I can even now hardly understand my boldness, but as I made my farewell I kissed her lightly on the cheek. "Thank you," she said, with feeling as though she was thanking me for my past services, and indeed she was as the emphasis on her thanks implied. I left in a sorrowful mood.

When I met Lord Carleton at the appointed time he was in a state of some excitement instead of his usual calm. Nevertheless, he first discussed with me the notes I had sent to him on my visit to Berlin. He urged me not in any way to speak about my view of our Ambassador there, though he said confidentially that at the Office they were beginning to an extent to share my opinion. He had however discussed with his colleagues the comment I had sent about the mood in Berlin concerning German interest in Africa, and reported that such comments had been received with interest, especially as they confirmed information received from other sources. On my legacy from Mrs Warburton he remarked almost casually that such a country estate ensured that I could sustain a higher social position, a remark that I did not understand until I has seen the Foreign Secretary.

We then went to the Office, not to his own department but to the Foreign Secretary's splendidly large room with wonderful windows looking over the park. I had of course expected to be thanked and was not surprised to be welcomed warmly. The Foreign Secretary was direct and sparing of words as always.

"You will be aware, Lackland, that Lord Carleton here is going to St Petersburg as Ambassador."

"Yes, sir."

"Therefore I need a Russian specialist at the Office."

"Yes, sir."

"You have all the right qualifications and I hope you will join us."

"Of course, sir. I will be honoured to serve here."

"As a minister, of course."

I could not quite follow him. I remained silent.

"That entails, of course, that you will have to go to the Lords, if you will agree to take a peerage."

I was fairly confident of the quality of my successes on the Treaty, but I had not expected this.

"You do me too much honour, sir."

"Not at all. It is not only your exemplary executive work which has been so important to us, but also the way in which you handled events with the necessary judgement.

Your reports from Berlin are of the kind we require. And as for St Petersburg, the Grand Duke Paul has written to me reporting the Emperor's enormous satisfaction with your work in exposing the French plan. That alone could be said to justify your elevation."

I remained silent and he glanced at me.

"Good! I have already spoken to the Prime Minister who has obtained Her Majesty's approval. You can visit the College of Arms to arrange your title. It will be announced at the end of the week. Good Morning!"

Lord Carleton did not actually have to carry me out, but it almost amounted to that. He drove me home in his carriage, and on this occasion mentioned explicitly that events had more than justified his engaging me. Well, they had.

Aha! I would soon be Lord Lackland and a true colleague of the man now Lord Martinlake. I had brought some sweet champagne back from Russia and I would now insist that he pours it over me and licks it off.

THE END

More from Oleander Press, Cambridge publisher since 1960.

THE NIGHT CLIMBERS OF CAMBRIDGE – Whipplesnaith (Noel Symington) – First published in October 1937 and now a cult classic, recounting the courageous (or foolhardy) nocturnal exploits of a group of students climbing the ancient university and town buildings of Cambridge. A fascinating, humorous and, at times, adrenalin-inducing adventure providing a rare glimpse into a side of Cambridge that has always been enshrouded by darkness. Over 70 original photographs, digitally remastered. 9780906672839 HB 9781909349551 PB

ENGLAND, THEIR ENGLAND – A.G. Macdonell – A young Scot exiled to the alien landscape of 1920s England. 9780900891878

TEDIOUS AND BRIEF TALES OF GRANTA AND GRAMARYE – Ingulphus (Arthur Gray 1852 -1940) – The Master of Jesus College, Cambridge, writes spellbinding horror. 9780906672860

INNOMINATO: THE WIZARD OF THE MOUNTAIN – William Gilbert (1804-90) – A lost classic returns to the ranks of Victorian horror and dark fiction. 9780906672716

THE HOLE OF THE PIT (& By One, By Two and By Three) – Adrian Ross – Ross, a Cambridge contemporary of MR James, composed two impressive works of supernatural horror fiction which appear here together in one volume for the first time. 9780900891861

RANDALLS ROUND – Eleanor Scott (Helen Leys) – Scott crafted nine examples of the finest horror and super-natural literature ever written and never again wrote in this genre. 9780900891953

THE STONEGROUND GHOST TALES – EG Swain – An atmospheric collection of unsettling supernatural stories by E.G. Swain, chaplain of King's College, Cambridge, and a colleague and friend of M.R. James. 9780906672433

ZULEIKA IN CAMBRIDGE – S.C. Roberts – In 1941 S. C. Roberts (Master, Pembroke College, Cambridge) picked up Zuleika's tale – a short, piquant and hilarious sequel. 9780906672976

WALL AND ROOF CLIMBING (1905) – Geoffrey Winthrop-Young – Five years after successfully launching the original in the Night Climbing series, The Roof-Climbers Guide to Trinity, Geoffrey Winthrop-Young penned this astonishingly erudite parody of the literature guides of the time. 9780900891854

SELECTED POEMS - Xu Zhimo – The first English edition of poems by China's foremost modern poet Xu Zhimo, who studied in Cambridge in the early 20th Century. 9780900891694

COLLECTED POEMS - Rupert Brooke – 9780900891809

INSTRUCTIONS TO THE YOUNG BOOKSELLER - Ernest Heffer – The transcript of a fascinating, amusing and somewhat poignant address to apprentice booksellers in 1933 by Ernest Heffer, Chairman of the world-famous Cambridge bookshop. 9780900891960

Printed in Poland
by Amazon Fulfillment
Poland Sp. z o.o., Wrocław

LA SAINTE U
COLLEGE OF ED
THE AVENUE, SOU
6

WIT
LSU LIBRARY

14. NOV. 1972

# To and Fro the Small Green Bottle

THE MYSTERIOUS GREATWOOD
*Michael Clark*

THE KING'S ROOM
*Eilís Dillon*

THE YELLOW AEROPLANE
*William Mayne*

STEEL MAGIC
*Andre Norton*

CANVAS CITY
*Jenny Seed*

THE SUDDENLY GANG
SURPRISE ISLAND
PRISCILLA PENTECOST
*Barbara Willard*

THE CRUISE OF THE "HAPPY-GO-GAY"
MALKIN'S MOUNTAIN
THE THREE TOYMAKERS
THE TOYMAKER'S DAUGHTER
*Ursula Moray Williams*

*and many other titles*

LA SAINTE UNION
COLLEGE OF EDUCATION
THE AVENUE, SOUTHAMPTON

# To & Fro the Small Green Bottle

by J.B. SIMPSON

illustrated by John Lawrence

Hamish Hamilton

*First published in Great Britain 1971*
*by Hamish Hamilton Children's Books Ltd.*
*90 Great Russell Street, London W.C.1*

SBN 241 02072 7

Copyright © 1971 J. B. Simpson
Illustrations © 1971 John Lawrence

For S. A. Simpson

*To and fro the bottle goes*
*The bottle with the message in*
*But for the blurry message, still*
*Read "love".*

*Printed in Great Britain by*
*Northumberland Press Limited*
*Gateshead*

# Chapter I

MY NAME is George, and people tell me it's a good name to have, for there have been no less than six kings of England with that name. My second name begins with a D, but I'm not going to tell it. It's a daft name, and I don't know what my Mum and Dad were thinking of when they chose it.

The story I have to tell is a strange one, whichever way you look at it. Even my brother Arnold admits that. "It makes you think," he says, scratching his head, and our

Head Teacher Miss Worple always says it takes a lot to make Arnie think. But if you come with me to our school playground, that's where you'll see Arnie. Most of the boys will be kicking a football, and the one thing they have to remember at all costs is not to kick it over the wall. That's because Mr. Puffy Reynolds, who lives next door, pretends not to see any balls that land among his roses and lettuces. Who ever knew *him* to toss back a football before a quarter to four?

Arnie's that big, red-faced boy of ten. The little one in long trousers, with a big smile, that's my brother Willy. He is only five, and he can read nearly—fancy that! Only five and knows his letters! I can read, of course, but the problem is to find a book worth getting your teeth into. I read a good book once. It was about King Alfred and his jewel. I'd like to read it again but although I've searched the shelves, I can't seem to find it.

There are fifty-eight pupils at our village school when all are safely gathered. Now and then Arnie comes in late, because our Mum sends him off to the chemist at Towcester for her cough mixture. She doesn't like the chemist there, because he's cheeky. Then Arnie's face comes round the door, dark as a beetroot from running, his fair hair flopping over it.

"Hurry up and find your hymn book, Arnold!" cries Miss Worple, pounding the piano as we chant our song:

*"Though sun or moon*
*I may not be*
*To make the whole world bright*
*I'll find some little cheerless spot*
*And shine with all my might."*

Behind the high windows of the classroom, tall green branches heavy with leaves wave to and fro: "Shut your books and come outside, be with us, it's summer-time!" they seem to say. Little Dora Hopkins peeps at the teachers through a huge bright bunch of flowers she's brought for Emmy; Miss Emmy's our second teacher, the infants have Miss Clumper. "Sing up, all of you," cries Miss Worple. Anthony Bone opens his mouth wide as a whale's, to make us laugh, and a sweet he's been eating rolls right across the floor and lands beside the piano.

Down come Miss Worple's hands on the notes: bang! She swivels round to face him, and he stares back, trying to look brave and careless. Miss Worple doesn't speak, she just stares.

"What's all this, then? Have I arrived in time for two minutes' silence?"

The figure in the doorway is Captain Jenkins, Miss Emmy's middle-aged father, and all turn to look at him with a sigh of relief. It's always good when a visitor arrives, such a person carries away the teacher's interest, and leaves us to ourselves. Besides, Captain Jenkins is always a welcome visitor anywhere. He talks to us boys like we weren't boys at all, but friends of his. He has ever such good stories to tell. What's more, he is just the person to put Miss Worple into a good mood and save that show-off Anthony Bone from her cross outpourings. The Captain's round bright face is full of good will, and anybody can see he has something of interest to impart.

And now I will tell of something interesting that happened in our village, and it's true, not just idle gossip. In our village there stands a great house called Cuttle Hall. It is white and has huge big windows and loads of steps

leading to the front door. Inside there are more than thirty rooms, great tall rooms, too, and some have statues in, and great big vases so tall you could hide inside them. Once upon a time Captain Jenkins lived there, and Miss Emmy lived there too. But then his old father died and Captain Jenkins said to himself, "What with paying so much for my old father dying, by the time I die, there will be no money left to keep the place together!" So he stepped aside, and calling his nephew over from Australia, gave *him* the place. This nephew is called Mr. Bob Bright. He is in his thirties. He has a moustache and he wears smart, checked clothes.

Captain Jenkins and our Head are chattering in the middle room, and as I am going to the cupboard I overhear a little of their talk. "Now my dear Miss Worple," says the Captain, "I have a surprise for you, and a jolly one at that. An old friend of mine in Paris wishes me to receive his daughter as a guest. She is preparing a book about England and is anxious to study life in a little English village. Now would some of your rascals like to entertain her in the school? They might even pick up a little French! I know there's no one readier than yourself for a lark, as a rule!" At this he lights up a cigar, at which Miss Worple hastily opens a window.

"Gracious me," she cries, "and when is the young lady coming? Fairly soon? I shall have to think what we can do." Suddenly she notices me hovering round the cupboard. "George Burtwood, what do you think you're doing? Good gracious, take a new pencil then, and be gone."

So I seize one, grinning at merry Captain Jenkins as I pass. Suddenly I seem to see him with a beard and a big white ruff, like the chaps in those dark portraits up at Cuttle Hall. I peeped through the window once, and there they were, with their curly locks and little sharp beards. Mind, Captain Jenkins is more rosy-cheeked than they (are those men ill, or something?) but he has something of their lordly presences.

I scurry back to my desk and pass on the news. "There's a French lady coming to Ditchlington! She might even give us lessons!"

My friend Rodney is pleased. But French ladies would be too smart for our village, he says. They are the best dressers in the world. Elizabeth Dunn says that French people wear black all the time, while Tommy Jenner once heard of a French boy who was given soap to eat as a punishment.

"Did he blow bubbles?"

"I expect the bubbles blew right across the channel."

"I can speak French already. Just listen—"

"Shut up, Mary-Anne! You think you know everything!"

"It's only thirty miles across the channel to France. My cousin took his moped."

"What, rode it across the channel?"

"French people eat frogs' legs for their flavour."

"You'd better look out then, Debby, you—"

"Children! What's all this chatter for? Get out your sum books at once and turn to page twenty-two!"

With a sigh we scratch our heads and resume our childish studies.

# Chapter 2

OUR MUM is looking pale, she has her feet up on a chair. She has bought a nice-looking cake at Bedeswell, and she tells me to sit down and eat a piece. It's got cherries inside. Our Dad takes a slice too, but just when he's enjoying it she says, "They say I'll have to go back."

Dad's mouth is full, he stares at her with round eyes. "What, into hospital again, Mary love? How long for this time?"

"Oh," she says, "not more than a few weeks."

"Will Aunt Bette be willing to come, do you suppose?"

"I expect so, if you ask her nicely," she answers, smiling. But when little William hears this dreaded name he sticks his head out from under the tablecloth where he's been hiding and climbs on to Mum's lap. "Narty Lady!" he moans, hiding his face in her dress and sobbing. She pats his head and sings to him. Every time she stops singing for a moment he takes his thumb out of his mouth and gives her a big nudge. Dad scratches his head and looks morose.

"I'd better go and see her right away. What shall I say?"

"Say what you like! She's *your* auntie!"

"No need to rub it in," Dad cries, then catching my eye adds, "She's a good one, really."

He believes that if he pretends our Auntie Bette is golden-hearted, we boys will treat her kindly when she comes.

"What about Cyril then?" Mum wants to know, but Willy won't let her talk. "Sing! Sing!" he orders, and because she is kind, she does.

*"Won't it be a happy meeting?*
*Won't it be a happy meeting?"*

"Not with Auntie Bette it won't," I mutter.

"Cyril can get his own porridge for a change," says Dad.

Cyril is Auntie Bette's lodger. He is a night-watchman. All night long he snoozes by one of those buckets of hot red coals, and all day he snoozes in front of Auntie Bette's fire. He is fat and greedy. Auntie Bette, on the other hand, is just the opposite. She is as thin as a match and she seldom sits down because then she would have to stop scrubbing. She is tall as tall, but carries her head low, so as not to bump into doorways.

When I break the news to Arnie up in our bedroom he nearly throws his Shakespeare out of the window. Once Arnie found Captain Jenkins's pipe in the long grass by the bus shelter and Captain Jenkins gave him this huge red volume of Shakespeare's plays as a reward. I know which part Arnie is reading. It is the part in *A Midsummer Night's Dream* where five old men are rehearsing in a wood. Arnie plays one of these old men in our school production, and as well he plays a roaring lion. Arnie roars and roars fit to kill at home, but when he gets to school, he comes over all shy. "Roar up, Arnie!" Miss Emmy has to beg.

"If she's coming," Arnie warns, "I'm off," and he locks his Shakespeare in his small brown suitcase.

"Watch your step, now, Arnold!" I say, borrowing our auntie's bossy tones.

"She ought to be in the army, ordering people about," says my brother bitterly.

"Don't forget she sent me that postcard."

"What postcard?"

"When she was on holiday in Bournemouth."

"I never saw it."

"You did, because it was a view, and you said the sea looked slimy."

"Oh well, if I said that, I expect it did," says Arnie.

Rat-tat-tat!

Guess who's at the door, wearing a brown hat with velvet loops and carrying a bag of cleaning stuff? Yes, it's

Auntie Bette. "You've saved our lives, Bette!" says Dad, giving her a kiss. Soon afterwards he goes to stay at his brother's house in Bedeswell. He pretends this is so he can be near our mother, but anyone can see who it is he's dodging.

Our Aunt has these sharp ears and often she hears us talking: "You shouldn't use that word, George," she complains, and "Where are your please and thank you, Arnold?"

Arnie says he will learn a foreign language, so as to trick her.

"You can learn French from Mam'selle What's-her-name."

"Pooh, I don't believe she'll ever come!"

"She will, Miss Emmy says so. Go on, Arnie, remember it's swimming tomorrow!"

At this Arnie cheers up rather. Swimming is his favourite sport. I like it too, but I don't swim very well. Most of us look forward to Wednesday afternoons in summer-time when the big coach swings down the hill, and carries us off to the baths at Leadenhall.

It's hot next day, and we children stand fanning ourselves with chestnut leaves as we wait near the village green. Oh for an ice-cream! Oh for cold water!

"Here it comes!" cries Mary-Anne and for once she's right. The big blue coach stops with screaming brakes, and in we jump.

Off it rolls, carrying us to our destination. Soon we are undressed, and flying over the short grass, waving our arms and shouting. But near the water we pull up short. We gaze alarmed at the cold green bulk of water, so inviting and yet so sly. In goes one toe—then another.

Fancy, girls are often better than boys, when it comes to swimming! That's because they are more fat. Their fat keeps them afloat. In goes Mary-Anne, the show-off of the school, then Mary Stokes, then Elizabeth Dunn—splash, splash, splash—"Right!" shouts brave Arnie, and in he goes after them.

It's cold! Only at first though, after a moment the water feels like silk wrapping round you. Rodney is shivering and green, but he finds a penny lying on the bottom of the pool. "Yes, Rodney, you can keep it," Miss Emmy tells him. She stands at the edge of the pool, watching us. She's a life-saver, and if one of us sinks she'll jump in and pull him out.

Miss Emmy was born in our village, and when she was a little girl she grew up at Cuttle Hall, which people say is haunted. I say so too—but more of that anon. Miss Emmy's mother and father were kind to village people, and when they grew peaches and strawberries, they'd let people buy them cheaply. Every Christmas they'd have a big tree for all the children in the village.

Miss Emmy doesn't live there any more. She lives in a little cottage with her father. Myself, I'd rather live in a cottage than in that big haunted place, with dark trees growing round it, but Mum says Miss Emmy was sad to go. It was her home, after all, and home is where the heart is. And sometimes on summer evenings I see Miss Emmy walking past her old home and gazing at it. She goes with armfuls of flowers to the churchyard, past the munching cows in the meadows, and through the iron gates to her mother's grave. I see her when I go to get lettuces for my Mum from Crusty Clarke, the new gardener at Cuttle Hall.

Crusty is stingy, and never lets things go cheap. He is Bingo-mad, but there, as my Mum says, what else has a hard old bachelor like that got to live for?

The girls are playing a swimming game, it's a sort of tag:

> *"Eeny meeny macca racca,*
> *Bet I catch the first and smack her—"*

"Race you to the end of the pool!" Rod calls. But I don't answer him. I'm watching something. Across the green grass a lady is running; a big lady in a black bathing costume. All of a sudden, SPLASH! she is in the pool.

Fancy that, a stranger amongst us children!

Up and down the pool she goes like a sea-lion. Then she turns on her back and shoots across the water like a cork. She is laughing and jolly. Suddenly she stands up straight. "Which of you is Emmy Jenkins?" she wants to know.

"It's I!" calls Miss Emmy, laughing from the bank.

"Oh! You are not in the water! Your father said I would find you in the water!" And she plunges about like a grampus looking for the ladder, then, finding it, climbs up and joins Miss Emmy.

It is the French lady, Mam'selle Drouet, in our midst at last.

As we jog back to school again I stare at Elizabeth Dunn's long wet golden hair, which looks like pressed-out corn, and it makes me think about a film I saw on telly. "Did you know," I ask Rodney, "that you can find gold in Australia?"

"There's gold in lots of places."

"If only Mr. Bob Bright would go to Australia searching for gold! Then he'd leave Ditchlington and Miss Emmy could go back to live in the Hall. Think what a squash it will be with Mam'selle in their cottage. What if she doesn't like dogs?" (Captain Jenkins has seven dogs, all yappers.)

"We could send a telegram," said Rodney, "saying 'Gold found on your land'."

"I wonder if there's gold in our village?"

"There's gold all over the place."

"When there was the gold rush," I tell Rodney, "people stopped shaving and doing what they was doing, and left things in the oven, and kettles boiling, and just dashed off like they were, to dig for gold. Even on freezing days they climbed and climbed, and trudged on the ice, and gave up everything else to reach the gold place. And just with a little jam jar of gold, they could be rich enough to take a whole bath in champagne!"

The French lady is laughing away, "Ah," she cries, "these lovely children! They are so beautiful; the boys also!"

"You got here very soon!" says old big-eyed Mary-Anne.

"I came by fly," the French lady tells her.

"By fly?" Mary-Anne sits up and stares. Then the French lady stretches out her arms and makes zooming noises.

"Oh, by *air*," says Mary-Anne, nodding her head.

# Chapter 3

"SO YOU are all acting a play for us to see!" cries Mam'selle Drouet, "and what is this about?"

She stands in our classroom beaming at us. Rodney whispers to me that her ring is made of real diamonds.

"I know your Shakespeare well," says Mam'selle, "in France, we bow to his name. But what is this dream which a person has? I think it is soon Midsummer, and perhaps we shall all of us dream strange dreams!"

"It's about a king," says Tommy Jenner, he plays the part of King Oberon.

"It's all about fairies," screams Mary-Anne, who plays a fairy.

"It's about a naughty spirit!" I interrupt, for I have this spirit's part.

"It's about an old man who turns into a donkey!" calls Henry Robb, for he has this old man's part.

"Fairies? Spirits? Ah, Bravo! Then it is exciting!" Mam'selle's eyes shine and she smiles and waves her hands about. Then she asks for the oldest, biggest person to tell the tale. This is Tommy Jenner, so the rest of us pipe down.

Tommy Jenner giggles and goes red, then he calms down, although he still keeps fidgeting with his ruler. "Well you see, it concerns a fairy king, who decides to punish this fairy wife of his. They've had a quarrel. The real play, which Shakespeare wrote, that's got a lot more love and stuff in it, but we only do about the old men and the fairies. It's jolly good. When—"

"Oh, get on with the *story*," moans Mary-Anne.

"I am getting on, Fatty! Well, this King Oberon, he calls his servant Puck and he says 'Find me a flower called Love-in-Idleness'. Puck fetches it, and Oberon, he says 'squeeze the juice out on my wife's eyes while she is asleep. When she wakes up, the very first thing that she sees, even if it's a bear or a wolf or a bull, she'll fall in love.'

"So off goes Puck to find Titania. But first of all he sees these funny old men rehearsing in a wood. They want to act a play called *Pyramus and Thisbe* in front of the Duke Athens on his wedding day. This *Pyramus and Thisbe* it's all love and stabbings, and one of the old men has to dress up as a fair young lady, and play Thisbe's part, and speak in a little squeaky voice. Another one has to take the part of a lion, and roar. This old weaver called Bottom, he wants to play all the parts himself: 'I'll be the lion,' he says. 'I'll roar like any nightingale!'

"They don't see Puck watching, because he's invisible. Only Oberon can see him (and the audience, of course).

"So Puck plays a trick. He fastens a donkey's head on to Bottom. This gives all the old men a fright. They run away. Then Titania who is asleep quite near, wakes up and falls in love with this old Donkey man. Of course the play ends happily, ours does, and there is dancing and stuff, and pretty songs."

While Tommy's talking I think about Puck's part. I wouldn't want to play a sort of spirit normally, but Puck is different. He's ever so mischievous. He jumps into old ladies' beer mugs and flies in the wind, and rushes round the whole world in forty minutes. He can turn into anything he likes; he can vanish, if he wants.

As for the magic flower, why, I gathered it myself. I found a little mauve one near Cuttle Hall. Nobody ever saw one quite like it before, and even Miss Worple can't find its name in any book. When I squeezed it, lots of juice came out, so I picked another and another, and I put all the flower juice in a little green bottle with some oil in to stop evaporation. It has a smell which you like at first, then it seems too sickly and sweet. I took the bottle, and I hid it away carefully. Just as well with

Auntie Sharp-Eyes round the place. She has this habit of throwing things away. Already Arnie's catapult has gone. As for scrubbing, why, I do believe if the world ended and all was smoke and sulphur, Auntie Broomsticks would be out on a bare mountainside looking for something to scrub!

She does a good bit of talking as well as a good bit of cleaning, and this is her chorus: "Is your neck clean? Are your nails clean? Just *look* at your shoes!" Arnie's mood has gone from dark grey to black since her arrival. He takes her name in vain terribly. I remind him of what Dad said once to us—that her true trouble is this; she has had no love in her life.

"Love!" Arnie hates talk of this sort. He makes the worst of his rabbit faces. He says he would like to land our auntie on the moon, with no equipment.

"I know what, Arnie! I'll squeeze some magic juice on her eyes. Then she'll wake up and fall in love."

"Why, she might fall for Will's tortoise! Then she'd go rushing after it—"

"She wouldn't have to rush, not after a tortoise."

"*Mine eyes do love my ears do love thine voice, my eyes thy shape!*" I sing. These are the words Titania uses in our play, and Arnie smiles a little, forever fired by his hero Shakespeare. "Go on, then," he says, "let's have some more."

"All right! '*Be kind and courteous to these gentlemen—feed them on raw cabbage leaves and my dreadful cooking—*'"

Auntie Bette is a bad cook, and as well she has this mania for raw cabbage. She says it wards off colds. I'd sooner have a cold, than have to swallow that tough bitter stuff.

One evening it's raining, and we boys decide to have a game of marbles. Soon Auntie Bette walks in, and treads on one just as it's rolling by—down she comes with a wallop. She sends us off to bed. There is no light in our room, because our aunt took the bulb out. She says Arnie reads too much. Arnie is more raving than ever. "Some people don't deserve love!"

"Love might transform her."

"Transformed or not, she would still be here."

"She might follow her heart elsewhere."

"Her heart!"

"She must have one, Arnie, or she'd drop down dead."

Later I lie in bed, gazing over at the window. It's a clear night, full of stars, and I can't seem to sleep. The moon is white and bright. It shines steadily in the darkness, where all our clothes and toys are scattered, and fills the room. I think sadly of our Mum in bed in hospital, where everything is kept so neat and white. With a sigh I get up and tidy things a bit. Then I say my prayers. *"God is the branch, and I the flower—the Lord my soul I give each hour—"* I mention Mum, and her chest, and I ask blessings for Miss Emmy and one or two others. First I leave out Auntie Bette, but later my conscience pricks me, so I add her name to the list.

"Twit—towhoo—towhoo—"

How long did I sleep? What time is it now? The moon's gone, but it's night time still and William is snoring. His adenoids should come out. "Arnie!" I call.

There's no answer. All at once I have that strange feeling as if something odd is about to happen. When I sit up and stare into the thick darkness, I can hear my heart thumping like a stick. There must be a strong wind, for our little white curtains are waving at the windows. "Arnie!" I call.

But my brother's bed is empty.

Where is he? Whatever's he doing?

Then all of a sudden there's somebody shaking me, and somebody banging my shoulder. "George, George, wake up!"

I shrink back, staring up at the figure in stripy pyjamas. "Arnie, it's only you!"

"Get over then," he says, and pushing me over he

jumps into bed beside me. "Guess what, George! I anointed her lids! Just like you said!" His teeth are chattering, but I know he's grinning. I sit up and take notice.

"You did *what*, Arnie? *What* did you say you did?"

"Don't pretend you can't remember, George! You told me to do it! You said she needed love, so I put some of your juice on her eyes. She was asleep, so I just sort of sprinkled it on."

"Sprinkled it on *who*?"

"On Auntie Bette, of course."

"All of it?" (This flower juice is precious to me. I keep it in a little green bottle where my mother once kept scent.)

"You didn't use it all?"

"Of course I didn't!"

Arnie gives a sniff. Even in his pyjamas he seems proud and reckless, although he's shivering.

"You're mad, Arnie! Fancy daring! Why, what if she'd awoken! *Oh sleeping beauty I have here a love potion for your fair lids*—" I sway to and fro and bow and play the fool, and soon we are both doubled up with laughter.

Later we creep downstairs and search the larder. There's nothing much there, but we take some slices of bread, and Arnie and I munch them happily, from time to time licking our fingers in lordly fashion.

Next day there is not a cloud to be seen in the sky, and the hot sun pours down. As Arnie and I saunter home from school, we are like two scones newly taken from the oven. We agree to go down to the river. Old Mr. Puffy Reynolds is out in his garden in his shirt sleeves, hoeing among his bright flowers, his transistor blaring by his side. "It's a scorcher, boys!" he cries. He's in a good mood just for once. Anthony Bone is doing burn-ups on his bike—up the green he goes and down again, up and down, a red iced lolly in his hand. His granny bangs on her window, watching him, but he takes no notice. As the big pie van passes us, we flatten ourselves against the grassy bank near home, and I whisper to Arnie, "Do you suppose she's in love?"

"Seeing believing," says my brother, grinning.

"Auntie gone." It's our big-eyed little Willy hanging over the gate.

"Gone?" cries Arnie, "gone where?"

"Gone for always," says Willy happily. I seize him and Arnie dashes past us into the house. As a rule old Sour-Face is at bay behind the door, wanting to know what we learnt at school and warning us to wipe our feet. But where is she today? A little breeze blows through the open window, but there's no note on the table. We run up to her room. The room is empty. There are no slippers under the bed, and on the door her thick brown dressing gown no longer hangs.

"Well there we are," says Arnie, and I know he is trying to sound ordinary, "she's gone off somewhere, that's all. Probably she went to the shops. Come on then, don't lag about; we'll buzz off down to the river."

So off we go. We take glass jars, and lolling in the long grass we gaze into the wide river as it saunters past green banks. There are leaves down there, thick dark ones that move in the sway of the water, but fishes are too artful by half. "Look, hundreds of 'em," Willy cries, pointing at his jar, but they aren't fishes really, the things in his jar. They are sort of weeny acrobatic things which loop and somersault in the clear water like broken elastic bands.

"Do you think she'll be there now?" I ask Arnie as we trail home.

"How do I know!"

"Wait for me, wait for me!" Willy has found a broken bird's egg, he carries it in a hanky and keeps gazing at it.

She isn't there. There's still no sign of our disappearing auntie. No kettle on the stove, no brush, no broom, no nagging voice. "What do we tell our Dad?"

Arnie bangs down his glass jar so that water splashes out. He turns the tap on and cools down his face. In a voice muffled by a towel he says, "She'll be back. She's just off visiting, that's all."

"Auntie never coming back," says Willy happily.

"Magic's rubbish, anyway," says Arnie.

"You don't think it was the Juice? I mean, what if she *did* fall in love, and what if it was the postman, or a burglar even! Why, she might have set off down the road—"

"Go on! Just because of some silly old flower-juice!"

In three days all the food in the house is gone and we've spent our few pennies. Willy starts howling. He badly wants our Mum. My brother Arnie is red-faced and rabbity-looking. Why even our budgie looks miserable. As for me, for two pins I could bawl as loudly as a dog.

"I know, Arnie! We'll go and tell Miss Emmy and the Captain. They've got good hearts, and they'd never split on us."

Arnie scratches his head. I can see he is far from keen. "Very well, then," he says, "what else can we do?"

* * *

Miss Emmy and her father live in a cottage near the park. There are yellow roses on it and, as we stand there waiting for the door to open, these sweet, strong roses seem to me to smell a little like the flower I picked near Cuttle Hall, the very one from which I extracted the dread Juice.

"Hark, moosic!" Willy whispers, lifting a finger. Peeping past the curtains, I see fat Mam'selle a-swaying in front of the piano, and banging down the notes. Suddenly we hear footsteps. Arnie wants to run. I pull him back. "You say it then!" he insists, pushing me in front.

The door opens at last, and out of the darkness shines the round red face of Captain Jenkins. "By Jove! It's three of the lads. Not carol-singing already, are you? Bit early in the year for that, isn't it? Now if it's raffle tickets—"

But now here's our pretty Miss Emmy calling to us, and telling her father to stand back. She leads us into the front room, where we see Mam'selle sitting pounding the piano. The dogs start leaping about, and Willy clings to me— "They won't hurt you!" I whisper, and soon he is laughing as they lick our hands and faces.

It's ever so higgledy-piggledy in the cottage with flowers and books and pictures everywhere, and a strong smell of toast in the air. "Don't forget the diver" cries Chatterbox the parrot, and Willy shrieks with laughter. Captain Jenkins fetches a bottle, and offers us all a glass of wine, but Miss Emmy won't allow this: "I'll get some orange squash," she says.

Mam'selle turns away from the piano to ask if we know the tune she is playing. She tells us it is called the Marseillaise, and it is the National Anthem of her country.

"On important occasions such as this we play such a song."

Everyone is so kind and jolly that we almost forget the awkward reason for our visit. As well as three glasses of orange squash Miss Emmy brings huge slices of creamy cake. Mam'selle nods—"Me, it is my making!" she says. Springer, the brown and white spaniel, has a new trick; Captain Jenkins balances a lump of sugar on his nose, and there he sits quite quietly until he gets the words "Carry on eating!" from his master. Then he throws it into the air, catches it, and gobbles it down.

"And now," says Miss Emmy, "tell me something, George! Is this just a friendly visit, or had you some very special reason for coming?"

"Well—" I look at Arnie, but his face is near enough to rabbity to warn me he isn't going to be much help. So I explain, as best as I can, the mysterious absence of our auntie. I don't mention Arnie's tricks, nor how he sprinkled juice on Auntie Bette's eyelids, for such things suddenly seem too strange and daft.

Miss Emmy listens with her head on one side, full of sympathy. Then she goes and fetches us more to eat. "So it's a case of *Cherchez la femme*!" cries Captain Jenkins, "or don't you want to find her?" We look at him blankly. Then he tells us that *cherchez* means "look for" in French. "Well," Arnie explains, "we don't know where to cherchez."

Then suddenly Mam'selle brings her hands down on the piano with a crash. "It is good, it is good," she cries. She, she has a good idea; *she* will come and look after the little boys! "Me, I will be your aunt!" she says.

We stare at her. Captain Jenkins takes a long and

thoughtful swig from his glass of red wine. "Are you serious, Pierrette, my dear? Are you joking, or do you feel ready to care for three little waifs and strays for a day or two?"

"Indeed, I do not joke me! I love you, my dear friend Captain, I love you, my dear Emmy, but the little dogs—" and she looks down at the yapping creatures with an expression no nicer than some of Arnie's, "the little dogs I do not love. Plof! So many little dogs. But with little boys I am happy. I have brothers by me in France. Come, my children, will you take me with you? Will you lead me to your house?"

She holds out her hands, and we nod gladly. Then she goes off to pack, and I go over to the table where Miss Emmy is twisting flowers and pieces of wire. She is making the wreaths for the fairies to wear on their heads in *A Midsummer Night's Dream*. She smiles, biting a piece of cotton off and looking at me out of the corner of her eye. "Mind you look after Mam'selle now, George!"

"I thought *she* was going to look after *us*!"

"Well, I expect it will be half-and-half."

"What shall I wear on my head when I'm Puck?"

"I hadn't thought of that. You certainly won't want a wreath with flowers on, will you? What about leaves?"

"We'll have to be careful it doesn't blow off. I mean, Puck travels so fast, doesn't he? Even spacemen don't circle the globe in forty minutes."

"He ought to have a crash helmet."

"What, Puck take care? You'll have him taking out an insurance policy next."

"I could wear a wig. A big flappy sort of wig."

"What about a hair net," says she, "fastened under the chin? Just to keep your hair on, Georgie Burtwood."

# *Chapter 4*

MAM'SELLE SETTLES down happily in our little house. She sings and smokes all day long, and she reads lots of books. Often we hear her laughing away over these books. Her white hands with rings on look all wrong in the washing-up water, but she doesn't seem to mind, and we help her all we can. When our Willy cries she is just like a mother to him, she takes him up on her big lap and sings him little songs.

One of these songs is called *Il etait une Bergère*. It is about a little shepherdess who took some goat's milk and made a big cheese. Her old cat was watching her make the cheese, and when her back was turned he quickly ate it, so she fetched him a big smack. This little song has a chorus like this: *"Et ron ron ron, petit patapon!"* After Mam'selle has been singing this song for some time she tells us to join in the chorus:

*"Il etait une bergère—*
*Et ron, ron, ron, petit patapon,*
*Il etait une bergère—*
*Qui gardait ses moutons, ron ron, qui gardait ses moutons."*

Willy loves this song, and when we sing he gets quite excited.

Mam'selle doesn't eat much, perhaps she is on a diet to make her thin. "Don't you like eating breakfast?" Arnie asks one day, as she sits drinking a cup of black coffee.

"*Plof*" she says, or something of that sort. Willy watches her over a big spoonful of porridge. When he has finished, he wipes his mouth carefully, and then stands up on a chair looking all polite and important. "Mam'selle!"

"Yes my sweet cabbage?"

"Listen."

"'*Il etait une bergère—*
*Et ron ron ron petit patapon ron ron ron ron ron—*'"

He smiles away, pleased as a new pin with his squawky voice. "Bravo, bravo!" cries our French auntie and seizing him she gives him a great big hug.

When I tell Rod that the French lady has come to live with us, Miss Worple is standing close by, and she must have heard me, for she says in surprise "Is Mam'selle Drouet really staying at your house now, George?"

"Yes Miss Worple."

"Fancy that! Good gracious! Is your aunt there too?"

"No Miss Worple. She—er—she left rather suddenly."

A blush comes across my face and I run off to join Rodney quickly. "I believe Teacher thinks I've done Auntie Bette in!"

"So where's the body, man?"

"Oh get away with you!" Rodney runs off, but I catch him and fetch him a light punch or two. He punches me, and then we make it up.

Although we aren't very fond of Auntie Bette, it comes as good news when our Dad tells us she is safe and sound. It seems she suddenly started worrying about Cyril. So off she went, bag, baggage and all, to check up on how he was.

"What set her worrying, I wonder?" I say, catching Arnie's eye.

"It seems she had a dream one night. She dreamt that Cyril fell down a manhole, and was eaten by rats."

"Ha, ha! More likely that Cyril would eat the rats."

"Now then, boys! Well, so off she went, and there was

Cyril moping by the fire with a terrible stomach ache, and there was nothing to eat in the house, only ketchup. So she decided she must stay and look after him. I never thought your auntie cared so much for poor old Cyril," our Dad admits, shaking his head. "I always said she had a warm heart hidden away."

"Maybe something toasted it," says Arnie, glancing at me, and I know well what is in his mind. It is the power of the Juice. Why, how powerful it must be, if it can even make Auntie Bette dote on Cyril! And then I remember the little mauve flowers which cluster round the edge of Cuttle Park, looking so sweet and innocent. I wonder how Mr. Bob would feel if he knew their awful power. Just sweet little summer flowers, and yet they can soften the hard heart of a woman like our auntie!

"We live in a strange world," I say to Arnie.

"I wonder what she's feeding Cyril on now," says he. "He can't like that raw cabbage and stuff."

Mam'selle gives us smashing food, but I can see our Dad feels uneasy about the money she spends. Often I see him glaring at the things she has bought. She wanted to make a stew one day, and none of our pots and pans were quite right for her French stew, so off she went to Bedeswell and bought a fine red pot.

Dad went and took a look at it. He scratched his head. I saw her watching him.

"You don't like my *marmite*?"

"*Marmite*?" says he carelessly, not knowing that this word is the French one for stewing pot. When she explained this he said haughtily "Oh, it's very nice, I'm sure."

But she was a match for him. Planting herself in front

of him she said, "I will tell you something, Mr. Burtwood. A thing to make your mind happy. In the night when you sleep, who is it that comes creeping in? Just ask your son, with his Shakespeare! Why, it is the fairies who arrive. They arrive, they bring pots and pans, good things! They put them here. Then one day, they see it is time to go, so they take with them pots, pans, *marmites*—all that they have ever bringed. *Poof*! All is gone, like the wind!"

Dad has to smile, and so they shake hands both laughing:

"You win, Mam'selle!" says he.

Often in the morning you don't feel like getting out of bed. All cosy, you feel, as if you could stay there for hours and hours. You could, too, if you had laid in nuts and stuff, like squirrels do. Of course nuts might get monotonous. Squirrels don't seem to find them monotonous, but that's because they haven't tried ice cream and biscuits and pies; they haven't learnt about them.

Maybe it would be better not to learn about such luxuries, then you'd be content with nuts. Once you know about better things you want them. But often when I pass a big tree in winter, I think is there a dormouse in there, fast asleep? And then I think how dormice don't even know what day it is! Time for them comes in larger chunks. Great spells of sleep, really, till the spring.

Of course it's a bit like this for my Mum in hospital. She just lies there sleeping most of the time and she says she feels quite happy doing that. I like it when we visit her, but it's a bit sad, too. Willy doesn't come, he's too little, but our Mum lies there smiling up at Arnold and me.

She is still too pale, but she says she feels much better.

"You've grown, George! Even in two weeks! Fancy Auntie Bette walking out like that! Arnie, are you taking your chest mixture?"

Next to our Mum lies a very old person. She is so small and thin that you'd think the bed was empty if you didn't see her head on the pillow. She wears a pink knitted cap and she keeps reading the Bible out loud. *"Behold, I see a new Heaven and a new Earth!"* she reads. She's a nice old thing and she gives Arnie and me each a pink jelly sweet out of a little tin she keeps near her bed. I don't think she hears us saying thank you, as she is deaf.

We tell Mum all about Mam'selle and she seems delighted.

"What a kind person she must be! Fancy that!"

"She *is* kind," Arnie says, "jolly kind. And—Mum."

"Yes?"

"Um—" Arnie clears his throat and grows rabbit-looking; he throws me a glance and then, fingering the blanket over her, he says, "Mum, we want to ask you something."

"Go on, then, love!"

"It's about—well, you see, it's about the fair. Mam'selle wants to take us, and we want to go, but Dad says we must ask you first."

It's always a job to know what grown-ups will say next. Just when you think they're going to go off the deep end, they're ever so kind and friendly. Then it rains, say, and they find you've forgotten your mac, or some little thing like that, and up they go in a cloud of smoke.

When Mam'selle first mentions the fair, our Dad curses and moans.

"All that spending," says he, "And all on trash!" But

Mam'selle is pining to go. "It is the very bones of England," cries she, "the thing I arrive in time to see!" So what can he say then? Mam'selle has been so good to us, he can't be unkind now. To solve matters, he does the usual; he says we must ask our Mum.

"The fair!" Mum shakes her head. "They get awful big crowds there in Bedeswell. You might get lost."

"We'll be all right!" cries Arnie, bright-eyed. "She's ever so careful, Mam'selle is."

"What about Willy? You can't leave him behind! You must promise not to let him go on anything dangerous."

"Of course not. We'll hold on to him tight!"

"Don't let him touch any dangerous machinery."

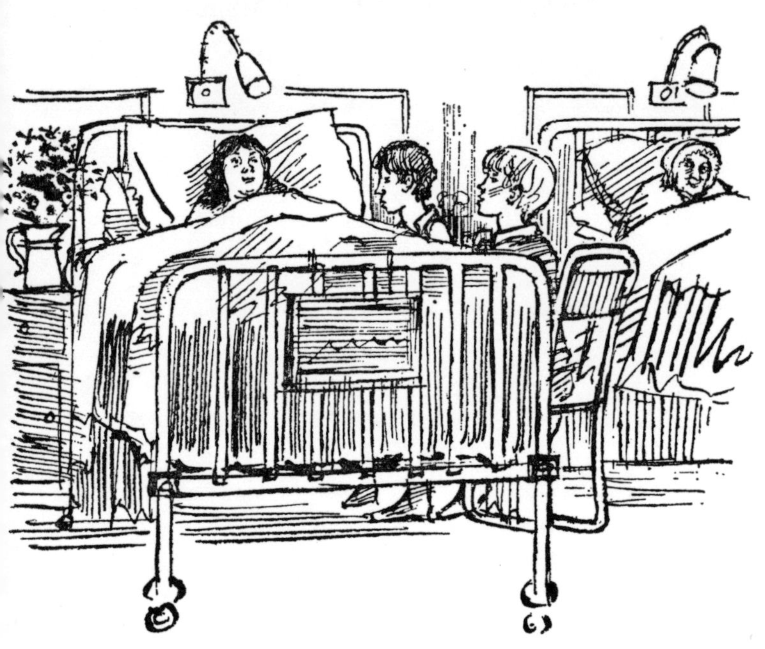

"Cross our hearts."

Our Mum looks up at us doubtfully from her bed. "Look here, Mum, there's no need to worry!" We sit and admire the flowers our Dad has sent along; yellow and mauve daisies, and some tight pink roses. The old lady in the next bed has been snoozing, but suddenly she wakes up and gives each of us another jelly sweet.

"Boys will be boys," says she, nodding.

"They will indeed," says our Mum, and that seems to help her make up her mind. "Very well, then, you can go to the fair, Arnie and George, but mind you be good boys now. Here, look, there's my bag. Take out five pence each."

"Oh, *thanks*," we say. "Thanks Mum, thanks very much!"

# Chapter 5

"ENCHANTING! OH, how it is pretty! We are in the land of the fairies! Ah, how my eyes are filled!"

We are wandering round the fair, Mam'selle, Arnie, Willy and I. Above us, the Big Wheel circles round like a heavenly chariot, and bright horses jump and sink on the roundabout. I feel the coins in my pocket. Mam'selle has given me fourteen. They are heavy, she says, and she wants to be rid of them. In France they don't have heavy money, they have money made of paper mostly. Mum gave each of us five pence, and our Dad added a ten-penny piece.

As darkness falls, the bright lights twinkle all the more and our hearts are light and gay. We have almost forgotten the shock our French friend gave us in the bus. At the time, my bones turned to jelly almost, and if the bus had turned round and gone straight back to Ditchlington, I would have blessed the driver outright. Mam'selle was full of questions on the way, and most of them were all right. "Who are those people? Why does that flag fly? How far is this Bedeswell?" Then suddenly she took us by surprise. "Look into my eyes, my little boys! Do they shine tonight?"

"Well, sort of—" We were not sure what she meant.

"You see, today I find George's magic bottle! So I sprinkle a little of the Juice first on the one eye, then on them both. So! Perhaps tonight I fall in love with an elephant."

Arnie's jaw dropped when he heard these words. "Didn't you hide it?" he whispered, giving me a nudge.

"Course I did!" As a matter of fact my latest hiding place for the dread Juice is behind a little china figure of my Mum's. It's a figure of St. Agnes, who is supposed to be a saint who guards ladies. (I like this little figure, even though it's chipped.) But now Mam'selle has found the stuff!

She is the only one we have ever told its secrets. She is a good one to tell things to, for she always listens, and she loves a good story. "So, the little arrow of Cupid falls on this little flower and makes it dangerous to the heart! It is the flower of love! Then I shall be careful, for I must keep my heart in one piece."

And now she's gone and dabbed some on! At first the thought takes the edge off our pleasure, but soon with the fun of the fair right close at hand, we forget the power of the Juice. Mam'selle wins an orange vase decorated with lemons, by throwing a ring over it, and Arnie wins a china squirrel by scoring under twenty-one with three darts. Next, Mam'selle wants a go with a gun. She misses the target altogether.

We wander through the jostling merry crowds and reach the dodgems. Mam'selle screams all the time in her little car and closes her eyes; "Where are my nerves!" she cries.

Good little Will wanders beside us, holding my hand tightly. I treat him to a ride on the roundabout, and he sits on an ostrich. Then Arnie and I climb on board the Big Wheel. Dizzily we circle round and it's just as if the bright lights of the fair go somersaulting after us—trees in the sky, and stalls on the ground; whirling, zig-zagging colours. It's like the old lady in hospital said: "*Behold, I see a new heaven and a new earth*!"

Mam'selle has gone and bought our Willy a big toy rabbit almost as large as himself. He carries it carefully, peeping through its white, floppy ears. "I got a rabbit!" he cries. "Mummy-lady boughted it!"

"Do you want to see a boxing match, Mam'selle?" Arnold asks, and I know he would like to see one himself. But she shakes her head. "Enormous men hitting the one the other? Certainly no!"

But this is what she *does* want to see; she wants to see the Amazing Snake Lady. There are pictures of the Snake Lady outside this tent, and it's quite enough to put you off snakes for ever. The lady lies there, and snakes and lizards and bats and other creepy things go crawling all over her.

Mam'selle seems fascinated by these pictures. She stares at them. "How beautiful this lizard!" she cries, pointing to a frilly-looking monster. A girl in a fancy get-up calls out "Walk up, walk up, a shilling to see the strangest sight in the world."

In goes Mam'selle, while I wait outside with our Willy. Arnie goes off to try and have a peep at the boxing through a hole in the tent. "Not going in, dear?" the girl in the fancy get-up asks.

"Not on your life!"

"The snakes won't bite you."

"Don't they ever bite *her*?" I ask, pointing to the picture of the Amazing Snake Lady.

"They *have* done."

SNAKE
LADY
RIFLE

"Coo, she must be brave! What are all the other animals like?"

"Well—there's an iguana (that's a sort of lizard) and a boa-constrictor. Then there's melon bats—flying foxes—"

"Fancy travelling round with that lot!"

"You wouldn't believe what a lot they eat." She sighed. "I have to feed them, too. You'd think it was Christmas every day for them. Monotaurs, now, they like hard-boiled eggs, snakes fancy chicken or rabbit, and Mr. Iguana likes grapes if you please! As for the bats, well it's nothing for them to knock off a pound of bananas at a go."

Old Miss White from South Crescent comes creeping by. I never expected to see her at a fair; fancy her leaving off peeping from behind those lace curtains of hers. "You here, George Burtwood?" says she, "and William? All on your own, too?"

"It's all right, Miss White," I say, "we have an adult in with the snakes."

"Ho," says the old lady, "so that's how it is. Well, let's hope the snakes won't bite her."

Arnie came back, whistling. "Is she still in there? She's been a long time."

Will began yawning. I pick him up, but he's heavy, so I set him down again, and let him lean against my legs.

"Listen, are you sure she's still in there?"

"I've been standing here, haven't I?"

"So you say."

"I expect she's found somebody to chatter to."

"Or been gobbled up by a snake."

As the minutes pass, we begin to worry, and at last the

girl in the fancy get-up gives me permission to go inside and look for Mam'selle.

Oof, it's stuffy in there! There's this very big glass case, and inside it is this pretty girl in a bathing suit, and would you believe it, there's a great python breathing all over her. She keeps stroking this python, which waves its big flat head about like a torch. There are some branches stuck round her and bats cling to these like leaves on a tree.

In the corner of the case sits a great big lizard. It must be the iguana. It doesn't blink, and it doesn't move. It just sits. It looks as if it's been sitting there for thousands of years. It looks as if it had seen everything in the world, and knew everything in the world, and didn't care a jot for any of it.

But does it know about Mam'selle?

For although I search every face in the tent, not one is hers.

"She's gone!" I tell Arnie. "She isn't there!"

"You see," he moans, "I told you to watch better!"

Now we go round and round the fairground, asking people if they've seen her. We ask the man with the guns, and we ask the man with the darts, and we ask the boy on the dodgems: "Have you seen a dark lady, a jolly lady, a tall foreign lady with red cheeks?"

"Sorry," says each, "I can't say that I have."

It's dark as dark, and by now all the shouting and carry-on round us begins to get on my nerves. I can't stand the people pushing past, and the line of young men and old ladies shaking charity tins like rattles.

Will is nearly asleep. First we drag him, then we carry him. There are other oddments too, to haul about.

Near one end of the fairground we spy a big yellow caravan. Painted on it are these words: "WHY WORRY? CONSULT SAM SAWYER, MAGICIAN AND LAWYER, YOUR FRIEND THROUGH THICK AND THIN."

Arnie and I looked at one another. Then gathering up our courage we go up to the caravan, pause a moment, and knock on the door.

An odd little chap answers. He's wearing a black cloth cap, like a sweep's and round his neck there's a spotted red scarf. While we are explaining the reason for our visit, he snatches off the black cap and dons instead a red one with a bobble on. "It's my thinking-cap!" he tells us. "Step in, boys! You can forget about paying me tonight. I'm a rich man."

What a place to live! It's like a little old posh front room. There are big vases of plastic flowers and there's a stuffed badger, and a stuffed bird, and there are hundreds of snapshots stuck on the crimson walls. There are fancy looking velvet chairs, all got up with bobbles on, and there's a carpet as thick as a book, but soft. I stare at the photos. There are chaps in top-hats, chaps in bowler hats, chaps in stripy bathing suits, chaps in sort of knicker-bockers—one is lifting weights, with a sort of tiger-skin wrapped round him, and one is arm-in-arm with a native warrior. When you look close, you discover an odd thing. Each one is the same chap, really, and that chap is Sammy Sawyer.

"So, boys," says Sammy, puffing round his little room and tossing cushions about, "it's been a good night, yes, takings have been good, yes, weather's been fine, yes, can't complain of weather, no, a slight breeze perhaps."

"We have lost somebody," says Arnie, "and we want—"

But Sammy doesn't listen. He's got hold of a pack of cards. He sorts them out, then throws the lot into the air and catches them, just as if they were a ball or something. "Take one!" he tells Arnie. "Don't tell me what it is."

Of course he knows just which one Arnie took. "Worth a million of your television tricks!" he cries. "Worth hours at the goggle-box."

"Excuse me," I begin, "but we wonder whether—"

"Where's my trumpet! There now, I've lost my trumpet!" Sammy starts scrabbling round the place. Then up comes a cushion and he brings out a big black trumpet. He puts it to his ear. "Speak up, speak up!" he cries—but next thing is, he's thrown it down again. Is it an ear-trumpet? And is he really deaf, or just pretending?

"Mr. Lawyer, I mean, Mr. Sawyer," Arnie says, eyeing him in dead earnest. "We've lost a lady from France. She must be here somewhere. Can you help us?"

For a moment Sammy stares at my brother. He seems to be thinking hard, and his grin has gone. Then gradually back it comes. "Lost a lady?" he cries, "lost a lady? She'll show up! Friends always come back. Ah, would that foes never did! And now, boys," he goes on, leaping about nimbly, "I should like to show you a new marvel! Watch me light this candle!" And taking a match from a precious-looking box, he carefully sets a tall green candle alight.

For a moment we stare at the little light. Then Sammy tells us to blow it out.

Arnie turns a furious look on me. I shrug my shoulders and blow. Nothing happens. "Blow, blow!" Sammy tells my red-faced brother.

Arnie sets his teeth. Then he blows too. Nothing happens. The tall flame burns clearly, not even dodging his breath.

"What a trick!" says our host. "Would you be surprised to hear that a trick like that came over to this country with Boadicea? *Before* Boadicea? When I say before her, I'm telling you that it was brought over by her messengers, wrapped up in a box the likes of which you never saw? Yes, the likes of that box you never saw! You never *will* see them," added Sammy sadly, "on account of antiquity swallowing the box. And now my dear chaps, I fear you have to go! Yes, a pity, but call again one day. No charge. What a night!"

Suddenly Sammy notices our worn-out Willy, asleep against a chair. "Ah," says he, "a baby, I believe. Was he here before? I didn't notice you'd brought a baby with you. Treasure him, gentlemen, treasure him!" and he bows.

"A nut," I say to Arnie as we breathe the wet night air.

"A nit, more like," says my brother viciously. "Your friend through thick and thin, indeed!"

"Fat friend he was to us, I must say."

"The tricks," admits Arnie sourly, "they were all right. I wouldn't mind being able to do some of those."

Back at the Snake Lady's tent, we find the girl in the fancy get-up counting out the cash. She keeps yawning. No, she says, sorry, but she doesn't remember seeing our French lady. Most likely she's gone back home.

"Perhaps she has," I say to Arnie, "we'll soon know." There's a radio blaring away somewhere near: *"I'm looking,"* sings a bloke, *"for a little glance from you."* I look at Arnie. His glance isn't the sort anyone would go looking for. His face is white and his eyes are desperate. "Come on," says he, "we'd better get the bus."

Lugging our Will and the rest of the stuff, we make for the bus stop. There we stand in the pouring rain. Len

Stewart from Towcester is there, cuddled up next to Mary Pike. "What do you think?" I ask Arnie.

"I'm thinking about Auntie Bette."

"You mean—the Juice again?"

"She said she'd smeared some on, didn't she? You ought to have hidden it better."

"But just because it's well, sort of love-juice, why should that make people *disappear*?"

"Auntie Bette disappeared, didn't she?"

"But why should love make people take to their heels?"

"Love!" Arnie's almost snarling by now. "Paah—it's not love—it's just—"

"Just what?"

"Just something quite ordinary."

I heave our Will into a more comfortable position and lean against a lamp-post. The rain's coming down sideways and it's running off my wet hair down my neck. "It isn't ordinary, Arnie, and that's that. Listen! Do you remember what Miss Emmy told us? She said that in far off times, in Shakespeare's times, people really believed in magic. She said people weren't stupider then, they weren't daft just because they didn't have electric lights and cars and that. She said that in those days, if you saw a fairy, people wouldn't send you to have your head examined. They really believed in bad fairies, and good fairies, and—and spirits, and that. Funny things did happen, and if you talked about them, people believed you. They didn't just say you were talking daft. You see this flower, this juice, perhaps it really does make you come over funny—"

"Great idea, I must say," grumbled my brother.

"We may have made a great discovery, Arnie."

"Fine! And remember our Dad's coming over Friday evening."

"Crumbs, so he is." Still the rain pours down and still our bus doesn't come. Number Eighty-four, that's no good, seventy-eight, that's no good.

"That girl from the snake tent, Arnie, the one counting money, she seemed to be looking at us in a funny way. I bet she knew something."

"We ought to have gone in and taken another look."

"She never would have let us."

"She looked odd, to me."

"She did."

"Here's the bus!" cry Len and Mary, and with heavy sighs we lug our Will on board.

# *Chapter 6*

*"'So the soldier went marching into town. Left, right, left, right! His boots took the high road proudly, for his pockets were heavy with money. Gold coins, silver coins—'"*

"Why, whatever's the matter, Arnie?"

Arnie jumps. He likes stories as a rule, and Miss Emmy is quite a favourite of his, but he isn't listening this time. I know why. She never came back. Our Mam'selle has gone and vanished, just like our auntie did. She went into the snake tent and hasn't been seen since.

What's happened to her? And what's our Dad going to say? I don't look forward to seeing him. It's Mum I should like to see. I should like to rush into the big hospital, tear up the great flights of stairs, never looking at anybody—rush past patients, and nurses, and trolleys, and never stop once till I arrived panting at the bedside of our Mother. Then I'd throw myself down and pour out my heart and tell her every bit.

The lead of my pencil goes, but I don't care. I can't seem to do sums. I feel so upset that when Willy comes through for a rubber and bumps into me I give him a pasting, even though he's littler than I am. This makes Miss Worple cross. "Ha, ha, ha!" gloats Mary-Anne, as I return to my desk after a good scolding. She's ticking all the sums in her book with a red crayon; what's the betting half of them are wrong?

While I'm trying to work out how many fourteens there are in thirty-eight, the telephone rings. Miss Worple waves her hand at us, telling us to be quiet, and I wait with my ears pricked. Could it be *her*? Could it be Mam'selle, ringing through to the school to say she is safe and sound after all?

But it isn't her. And now here's the Dinner Man banging down the big tins of dinner, and Mary-Anne reads out the chalked writing on the tins: "Ooh, roast pork! Jam tart and custard!"

My favourite dinner. But why should I care? I don't want to eat. I'm a server, as I lay the knives and forks and glasses out I'm sunk in gloomy silence.

By play-time, I know that if I don't tell somebody I shall truly burst. So I seek out trusty Rodney. I take him to a quiet place near the wall, away from the boys playing cricket, and I tell him he's got to promise never to breathe a word of what I tell.

"Not even to your Mum, Rod!"

Rod holds out his hands, pale and wise; "If I should split," says he, "may I drop dead."

Slowly I unfold the miserable tale. Rodney listens carefully, staring at me. At the end he gives me a great clap on the shoulder. "You're all right, mate!" he cries. "It's not your fault if she chooses to disappear, is it? People aren't like money, or something, which you can just go and lose through carelessness."

"She went into that tent," I say slowly, "and she never came out."

Mary Stokes and Mary-Anne Baker are skipping near us. Round fly the ropes, while the two of them sing their

little song. Mary-Anne has her eye on me, the minx:

> *"Wallflowers, wallflowers,*
> *Growing up so tall*
> *We're all ladies*
> *Wish we never die—*
>
> *Except for Georgie Burtwood*
> *He's the best of all!*
> *So turn your backs, you saucy cats*
> *And say no more to me."*

"Clear off," I tell them.

"No we won't, George Burtwood, we won't, we won't!" Mary-Anne sticks out her head bossily and nods, as is her habit.

Rod and I walk away. "Was there a boa-constrictor in there?" he asks.

"I believe there was. Wait a minute. There was a python—"

"A boa-constrictor can gobble up a whole person quite easily. It doesn't have a jaw-bone, see. It has sort of pouches that blow out like bladders, and it's got one hundred and ten teeth."

I stare at Rod miserably. Oh how I wish Miss Emmy had never chosen *A Midsummer Night's Dream* for us to act! How I wish we'd none of us heard of William Shakespeare! As for Puck and his pranks, I'm sick and tired of them. I've thrown away the dread Juice, and filled the bottle with water, but I don't like dabbing even that on Elizabeth Dunn's eyelids. What if I mysteriously cast a spell on *her*? What if she went and disappeared, like the others? Why, the Dunns would never get over it, with her being so useful, and taking the baby for walks every Sunday.

"Can someone else have my part?" I ask Miss Emmy.

"George, whatever's come over you today? You don't want to play Puck?" She can't believe her ears. "Puck's a fine part, and of course it's yours, and you must do your best."

There's a big airliner flying overhead, drowning the singing and the voices as we rehearse in the big garden. I pick up mown grass and let it run through my fingers. Is the airliner going to France? What if the boa-constrictor ate Mam'selle? Will our Dad be home tonight? What's he going to think?

Suddenly Mr. Bob comes striding over the lawn. Miss Emmy is kneeling down watching the rehearsal; there's a bit of a wind, and her long fair hair blows about. Mr. Bob calls "Hello, you ladies and gentlemen!" and flashes his smile at us. Then he goes up to her and leaning down, whispers in her ear. He is a handsome man, and everything about him looks rich; even his smile. He looks like a man on telly.

*"Be kind and courteous to this gentleman,*
*Hop in his walks, and gambol in his eyes*
*Feed him with apricots and dewberries—"*

Titania has found her donkey friend, and thrown her arms round him. Henry always brings his donkey head to rehearsals. I bet he feels hot in that shaggy thing. The way he sees out is by looking through its nose.

"I say, am I interrupting the play?" asks Mr. Bob in a loud whisper.

"No," says Miss Emmy, watching the fairies dance off with their arms round the donkey, "we were going to stop for a moment."

Then she pushes back her hair and he helps her up. There's grass on her skirt, she brushes it off and turns to him smiling.

"Do you know the story of *A Midsummer Night's Dream*?" she asks him.

Seeing these two together, I remembered what Mam'-selle once said. "Zees Mr. Bob," she said as she clattered round the kitchen, "I do not understand him. This Cuttle Hall—it is beautiful, yes, but what *sort* of a man is he who lives there? Is he a savage? Or has he the *bon gout*?"

We giggle. We don't know what "*bon gout*" means. *Bongoo*, that's the way it sounds. Mam'selle brings out her tiny dictionary. "'*Gout*'—it is taste, it is an eye for pretty things, for order, for a proper way. Like your mother has, with her pretty china. Now, Mr. Bob, does he love this fine hall? Does he love the many treasures there? Or is all he thinks to himself, 'Ah, it is the same thing as many francs?"

"You mean, does he like the house, or just the money it cost," says Arnie through a mouthful of her good cooking. Even the way Mam'selle fries eggs and bacon, why, it makes them a truly lordly dish.

"I have the answer," Mam'selle stands there, feet well planted, waving with her hands like a band-conductor, "Let him marry his cousin Emmy! This is the best. Her father should arrange this. He is too lazy a man, he should think, *think*" (and here she taps her own brains with one finger) "yes—think about his little daughter. So! The marriage is arranged, the family is made one. Miss Emmy is in the place she loves, Mr. Bob has a wife—good!"

"*Her* marry *him*?" Arnie makes his worst rabbit face, like a rat's more, really. "Poor Miss Emmy having that meany for a husband." Mr. Bob found Arnie taking cherries once, and he made it tough for my brother, so Arnie told me.

Mam'selle pats Arnie's head, laughing. "Ah, the little boys, they are not romantic! But she will improve him. You will see. A good woman, she can model a man. A man becomes clay in her hands. Mr. Bob is not a bad man, I think, only a little stupid. But one prays he will get wiseness. For myself, I pray for wiseness every day."

"Do you get wiser, then?" Arnie wants to know.

"If not," says she, "then it is by the will of God that I am a fool."

When I think of all this, standing in the garden up at Cuttle Hall, I too pray Mam'selle's prayer. I pray that she gets wiser and wiser, till at last she comes rushing back to our house again as fast as her legs can go.

# Chapter 7

OUR DAD is a big man. He drives a gravel lorry, and often he goes for miles and miles; right up North, or right down to the West country. He looks tired when he comes in today. He takes off his blue shirt and starts washing in the sink. He covers himself in soap until it's like grey grease spread all over his body; then he asks Arnie to rub his back.

"I saw your auntie today." (Dad always says "*your* auntie" even though Auntie Bette is really *his* auntie, which makes her our great-auntie.) "Yes," says he, "she seems well enough. I told her the French lady had taken over here, and she tossed her head."

"Did she?" asks Arnie, scrubbing away.

"She did. So your Mam'selle is off out, is she? Well, I'm not sorry. She's a good sort, but I can't call the place my own with her about."

"No?" says Arnie, washing off the soap.

"She hasn't poisoned you yet, then?"

"No," says Arnie, being helpful with the towel.

Willy sits nearby, his huge white rabbit on his lap. "Nice Mummy-lady got big rabbit for me," he says. He calls his rabbit "Mish", because Mam'selle called it "M'sieur", and that sounds like "Mish" to Willy. He peeps out at our Dad from between its floppy ears; "Mish looking at you, Dad," he says.

"Well, now," says our Dad, once he's dressed tidily and settled himself down to a nice cup of tea, "I've got some good news for you boys. Your mother will be home in a couple of days' time."

"Three cheers!" we cry. "Mum back!"

"Your muzzer coming back." Willy tells his rabbit. But there must be something odd about Arnie's expression, for our Dad says, "What's up with you, old boy? Come on now, out with it!"

At which poor old Arnie bursts into tears.

Life is full of surprises. The very thing you feel so dark about one moment can suddenly twist round and show a smiling face the next. Our Dad doesn't go flying off the handle when we tell the story of our missing Mam'selle. Not a bit of it. He just says we are great idiots not to have told anybody before. "What, did you think you'd done a crime or something? Why didn't you tell Captain Jenkins? Or the police? What, are you scared of the police? Why, if they aren't there to help you, what do you suppose the country pays them for?"

He sits there sipping his tea quite calmly, and Arnie toots loudly into a handkerchief. "Besides, missing persons are quite a speciality down at the police station," says our Dad. "They've got boxes of them down there."

"Boxes Mish in purses," Willy tells his rabbit.

"Boxes of them?" asks Arnie, staring at our Dad. We've both of us moved nearer him, so as to be able to listen carefully.

"Boxes of names, old pal. Sometimes people take it into their heads to vanish, see. They get fed up with their job, or their town, so they just clear off and start again somewhere else."

Our Dad sits there in his fresh white shirt, stirring a cup of tea. "All the same," he admits, "there have been some odd goings-on lately. And I'm not suggesting this French person cleared off in the above manner. But there's your Auntie packing herself off, and now this French lady—you've been good boys I hope? Not up to any mischief?"

"Auntie Bette isn't missing though," Arnie points out. "She's gone back to Cyril."

"Yes. But that's an odd thing too. A short while ago she hadn't a good word to say for Cyril, now she's eating out of his hand!"

"This village must be bewitched," I say to Arnie as we set off for the shop for Dad's tobacco. "Think of Auntie Bette eating out of Cyril's hand! '*Mine eyes do love thy shape, mine ears thy voice—*' "

"Never pick another of those flowers, Georgie, not as long as you live," my brother warns, and I grab a handful of buttercups and chase him, and he comes after me with some mown grass. Later we run into Tommy Jenner, who's got a wheel twisted on his go-cart. Arnie fixes it for him, and we both have a couple of rides. In such a fashion time flies by, and when we reach home we find our Dad has already fetched a policeman and is telling him about Mam'selle. The policeman is quite cheerful; he says that in his opinion the lady has probably returned to France and we shall hear from her quite soon. He knew a Frenchman once who was very sudden in his ways. Of course we don't speak about the Juice, but just as he is putting away his pen and straightening up to go, I ask, "Did you ever come across a case of magic, Officer?"

"Magic?" he asks, making his eyes go big as saucers.

"You've got us coppers wrong, old boy! It's facts we deal with down at the station, not fancies."

"I should think so too," says Dad.

Now we get busy making the house clean and tidy-looking for our Mum's return. We get going with dusters and brooms, and even little Will does his bit, rushing round with a brush and shouting "Away with you, dirt! Get away dust!" But soon he gets tired of work, and later we

find him fast asleep on the back door step in the evening sun.

Dad goes to fetch a bundle of washing from Rodney's mother, and as well he brings back a big bunch of flowers. Roses and daisies and all sorts, a big jugful to put in the window and gladden our mother's heart when she gets back.

# *Chapter 8*

THE STRANGE news about Mam'selle has spread round the village, and everybody is talking about it. Everybody wants to hear the story. The only person who seems really upset is Miss Emmy—but there, says she; there's no need to be really. Mam'selle is large, and sensible, and over thirty; she is not at all the sort to stand nonsense from strangers

"Well, you two are in a pickle!" Miss Worple tells Arnie and me after prayers. "Whatever happened?" And so we relate the strange story once again. "Well I never did! Good gracious me!" she cries, drinking it in. We take care never to mention the Juice. As Arnold says, we may as well be like the police and stick to facts, and not trouble ourselves with fancies.

"Poor Mam'selle Drouet!" our Head cries, "so where do you suppose she is? There's been no note? No message from her? Nothing at all?"

"No, Miss Worple. She just went into the tent with the snakes and was never seen again."

"But weren't the snakes locked up?"

"Oh yes, they were in this glass case, with this girl."

"Tch tch!" Our Head's eyes are bright. She loves a mystery.

*"You spotted snakes with double tongue*
*Newts and blindworms come not near*
*Do not harm our fairy queen—"*

Elizabeth Dunn is singing, she smiles: "I hate snakes!" she says, shivering.

"If your Mam'selle has been bitten, then she'll be stone dead," says Mary-Anne Baker, sticking her head forward and gloating. "Then you'll go to prison, Georgie Burtwood! So there and so there and so there!"

"Boadicea kept a snake," Tommy Jenner tells us, "I saw about her on telly. She was an ancient British Queen, and then Romans landed. She killed hundreds of these Romans, but there were too many. So instead of falling

into their hands she got this little snake to bite her. It was poisonous."

"You see! They'll hang you, Georgie Burtwood!" crows Mary-Anne.

"You don't know what you're talking about, Softy!" interrupts Rodney, "they wouldn't have truly poisonous snakes at a fair. Before they show these snakes, they take all the poison out of them. They can *bite* all right, but not poisonous bites. It would be like a sort of insect bite that's all, and the doctor would give you something for it."

Rodney always talks sense. He is thin and pale and reads books far into the night. He knows a lot about the world and I am proud to have him for my friend.

Tommy Jenner starts creeping about the floor, slithering to and fro. He gets Mary-Anne round the ankles. "Just you stop that!" she cries, her red cheeks growing even redder. She jumps up and down and sends her crayons

flying across the floor. "I'll tell on you boys!"

"Good gracious me, what are you children doing indoors!" shouts Miss Worple, who is trying to read a postcard. "Just you finish your milk and go out in the sun!"

The three teachers take their chairs and sit in a row in the playground. Miss Clumper, the infant teacher, is too soft-hearted; she blows her nose a lot and the kids can do what they like when she's behind her hanky. Just look at Henry Robb, now! He's chasing the girls with a spider in a jar! He runs round and round, making aeroplane noises. Mary Stokes goes across to complain. "Henry keeps chasing us, and spoiling our games!" she moans.

Henry doesn't notice that she's told on him. He just keeps chasing round making these wild noises. Our Head watches him. Gradually we fall silent and all of us watch Henry whooping and shrieking round the playground with his spider. There he goes, flapping his arms about and crowing like a bird.

Gradually Henry runs more slowly, as if he knows something is wrong. At last he stops, and looks round him, surprised. Then he sees our Head's eyes fixed upon him.

"Come over here, Henry."

He shuffles over. His eyes have gone all big, and he creeps up awkwardly.

"What have you got in that bottle?"

"S'only a dead spider," he goggles at her, innocent and fierce. "You see, they said I was—"

"I didn't ask what they said!" She takes the bottle away and looks at the spider. Everyone watches her. For a moment she sits there, as if considering what to do. A little wind comes over and Mr. Puffy Reynolds' washing in the garden next to the playground sways gently to and fro; whiter than white.

Our Head holds the bottle for a second, then suddenly she tosses the spider out at Henry. He moves back with a yell and everyone starts laughing. Even Henry has to laugh in the end. "And now get on with you! You leave the girls alone, in future!" she tells him.

"They said I was a—"

"Never mind what they said."

He joins the boys, grumbling. "I'll get those girls!" he says. Henry is a poor speller, and when he writes the word he spells it like this: "gyrrhls".

"Gyrrhls"! Even I know you don't spell girls with a "y".

# *Chapter 9*

OUR MUM is back home again. She is quite well again and we chatter happily for hours. She is full of questions. Did Auntie Bette do a lot of cleaning? Did she grumble about all the untidiness?

Mum is not a tidy person, she isn't for ever dusting like some are, Auntie Bette for instance. We admit that our Auntie said the place was "a real pigsty" but when I see Mum's brow grow dark, like Arnie's often does, I throw my arms round her neck. "But Mam'selle loves our house! She says you have lots of *'gout'*! That's a French word, and it means 'good taste', Mum. She likes the little china horses, and your picture of France! And she loves the flowery wallpaper upstairs!"

Mum starts looking happier.

"And how's Miss Emmy? Is she very upset about Mam'selle's disappearance? What does the Captain think about it all? And Mr. Bob?"

We shake our heads. We don't know. "But do you know what Mam'selle said, Mum? She said Mr. Bob ought to marry Miss Emmy, and take her to live with him in the Big House."

Our Mum's eyes sparkle. "That would be grand! Poor Miss Emmy, I'd love to see her at Cuttle Hall again."

"But what about Captain Jenkins?"

"Oh, he'd be snug enough in his little cottage. She

could come and see him every day. Besides he'd be happy anywhere, so long as he had those old dogs with him."

"Why do people keep having to *marry* people?" Arnie asks. He is making a model of an aeroplane: he squeezes the last out of a little tube of glue till his face grows purple.

"It's natural," our Mum says. "Everyone wants a person to share things with! Someone to talk to, once the kids are in bed."

"She could mould Mr. Bob like clay," I say, remembering our Mam'selle's remark, and for some reason this sets Willy off. He starts rummaging and searching and fumbling, and at last he brings from out of a brown paper bag a sort of clay model. It just looks like a kind of worm, and it's painted yellow.

"For you, Mum!" he says.

"It's lovely!" she says, taking it and he jumps on her lap, and there they sit, smiling at each other. "It's a snake!" he tells her, watching to see how she likes the idea, "it's a snake, Mum!"

Arnie and I reel back as if we've been shot. "Oh no, not a snake! Not that!"

"No, no, not that!" says Willy, shaking his head to calm us down, "not a snake, Mum, not that. It's a *griller*. It's a griller, boys." And he gives Arnie's arm a little pat, and nods at me, to comfort us.

The infants don't take part in *A Midsummer Night's Dream*. They are going to do a sort of stamping dance. Willy likes this dance, he is forever practising stamping. "What with you stamping and Arnie roaring," moans Mum, "this house is like a zoo."

Perhaps Auntie Bette's rudeness has nettled her, for late

one evening she starts tidying the kitchen cupboard. Suddenly she comes on the little green bottle. She picks it up and holds it up to the light. "Whatever's this?"

I made a grab for it. "Don't touch that, Mum!"

"Whyever not?"

"It was Puck's stuff. It was—well, you know, the *Flower Juice*. I've thrown it away, that's only water, but you never know."

She stares at me for a moment, then bursts out laughing. "Oh very well then, George, you keep it. I don't want Cupid aiming his darts at me, that's certain! By the way, is this little drop of tea all that we've got left? That won't last us long, that's certain. I tell you what, George, just you run up to the Big House and see if Mrs. Odger has got a packet out in her kitchen. Here's the money. Take care of it, now."

I ask Arnie to come with me, but he's too busy labouring over his model.

So I set off by myself.

The moon is up, and follows me, bright and clear in the summer sky. I go by Fox's Lane. It's called that because a Mr. Fox lived there once, not because there are foxes there—although there *are* weasels. I should know that. Once a weasel came out of the long grass, and it nipped my ankle—coo! I didn't see its face, but I felt the nip. So I don't go near the edge any more. I keep right to the middle. It's a narrow path, so I go carefully, beating at the long grass on each side with a stick.

I sing, too, hoping that way to keep off weasels.

There's a sweet and sickly smell floating in the night air. It's the tall lilies Mrs. Bone grows in her garden. They stand up straight and white as brides in church. I can hear Henry Robb roaring like a tiger and Mrs. Robb crying out "Just you stop that Henry or I'll—"

Fox's Lane is behind me, now; I'm out on the road. Danny the old white horse is blowing and stamping in his field. I open the little gate that leads past the church to the Big House, and there, through tall trees, I see it standing stately as ever, the house Miss Emmy likes so much. To me, such a place could never seem like home—fancy, all those rooms, and what a journey even to get upstairs to bed!

I don't go down the main drive, I go down the back way, past the stables and down a little winding garden path. Then I knock at the back door.

Mrs. Odger lets me in. She looks startled, and no wonder. It must be scary hearing a stray tat-tat on your door in a great place like that.

"Oh, it's you, George! Come in. Is your mother better?"

I say she is, and I ask Mrs. Odger about the tea. She's been busy making a fine pudding. It's set out on the kitchen table, all dabs of cream and chocolate and stuff. "Does Mr. Bob sit down and eat all that by himself?" I ask.

"No, no, but company's arrived, and he asked for something special."

"Any spoons to lick, Mrs. Odger?"

"I never leave any pudding on the spoon!" But she somehow manages to gather some upon a clean spoon without spoiling her fine dish. As I stand licking it Tanjy, the old ginger cat, awakes and stretches his long legs and eyes the pudding with interest. *"Will you love me, will you?"* sings a moaning voice on the radio and I go and give Tanjy a hug to show I love *him*, at any rate.

"You'd better give your Mum that tea then," says kind Mrs. Odger.

When I open the door, a great big moth swings towards me. It's just as though it's been waiting for me. Mrs. Odger waves it away, and I follow it through the dark, chasing the lovely thing as it zig-zags through the night, now here, now there, till at last it leads me to the front of the house.

Behind the huge windows there are lights lit and I take a peep inside. I love to see the portraits, and the rows and rows of books. When I notice Mr. Bob, I draw back hastily, but I can't resist taking a quick look at his guests.

It's then that my mouth drops open. I stand there staring. For isn't that small man Sammy Sawyer, the joker from the fair? And that lady with them, could it be—I blink, squeezing my eyes together tightly then opening them again several times; *could* it be—yes, it is! It's our own lost Mam'selle!

I have an effort not to call out. What, Mam'selle *here*, before my very eyes?

She isn't laughing and talking like the others are. She's quiet and hunched up in her chair. There's Sammy, now, dancing about and laughing, and there's Mr. Bob laughing too. Sammy has suddenly taken out all these pound notes and put them all over the table. Now he's produced a rope from somewhere. He gives it a shake—now, of all things, he's tying Mam'selle up! She isn't even struggling! As for Mr. Bob, he seems too busy counting the money to care. Now he's looking round. But he isn't going forward to rescue her. No—he's just standing watching. What is more, a smile is heartlessly raising the corner of his moustache.

What if they saw me? In sudden fright I duck down outside the window and start running. I go on till I've got the length of the drive behind me, and am well into the village. A minute later I'm pressing myself panting against the door in the village I trust most; the one which always opens to a friend.

*"Yap-yap, bow-wow-wow, woof-woof-woof—"*

"It's me, Miss Emmy! It's me, George!"

Here she is, bending to push away a rush of dogs. "Come in, dearie, do! Be careful of Fido, though. He's had a bite from Joey and he's very bad-tempered."

I follow after her, and she says, "Sit down, Georgie.

You're out of breath."

"I've just got to tell you something, Miss Emmy! I shouldn't have seen what I saw, I know, but I did," and quickly I paint the scene shown to me through that big window.

"I believe you're muddled up with something you once saw on telly, George!"

"I did see them! Honestly I did! It's true I saw them!" How can I make her believe me?

"It must be having to play the part of Puck. They do say actors get very involved with their parts. You've turned Mr. Bob into a villain, and Mam'selle into a—"

"You don't believe it's true?"

"Georgie—you know I like it when you tell me stories. But there are some which—well, one doesn't mind they're not being true. In fact one is glad they aren't. I wouldn't like to think Mam'selle was bound up in a chair like a lady in a thriller!" Miss Emmy shakes her head and smiles at me. "I know you've felt very worried about her. But you mustn't let your imagination run away with you."

I trudge home with a heavy heart. It's a terrible thing when nobody believes the truth. When, sooner than call you a great big liar, they good as tell you you've been seeing things.

But who *would* believe me? "What," they'd say, "Mr. Bob take a harmless lady prisoner? What, him let her be tied up in a chair before his very eyes, while he counted out the ransom money without a flicker?"

The only person who might understand me is my Mum. But you can't go telling alarming things to people who have lately come out of hospital. Then there's Arnie. But why drag *him* into it? Why not let him carry on as he is, all carefree, instead of blasting his life with misery?

"That's very nice, Arnie," I say, nodding at the model aeroplane he's making. Silently I give Mum the packet of tea. Soon afterwards I go upstairs and taking off my shoes, fall down on to my bed.

Arnie's Shakespeare is at hand, and I pick it up. It falls open at *A Midsummer Night's Dream*. I thumb through the pages till I come across Oberon's words:

*"Having once this Juice*
*I'll watch Titania when she is asleep*
*And drop the liquor of it in her eyes*
*The next thing then she waking looks upon*
*Be it a lion, bear or wolf or bull, on meddling monkey or on busy ape,*
*She shall pursue it with the soul of love"*

"Is there a clue there?" I ask myself. "What about Auntie Bette? Cyril can't have been the first thing that she waking looked upon, can he? What about us boys? Or didn't she get us our breakfast next day?"

I try and remember, but I can't.

*"Be it lion, bear or wolf or bull*
*She shall pursue it with the soul of love"*

I try and decide which Cyril looks most like of these. In a way, he's a bit like a small, sleepy bull. For eating habits, a wolf would be more the thing.

But Auntie Bette isn't a problem any more. It's Mam'selle who's the important one. It's hard to think *she*'s pursuing anyone with the soul of love. She didn't look as if she loved anybody at all, not the way I saw her sitting all hunched and miserable inside the Big House.

And what might be happening to her now? What might be going on, behind the tall trees, in that great dark house? Why, six long knives might be about to be plunged into her very heart this very minute, while I lie dreaming on my bed.

# Chapter 10

"ONLY THREE days exactly until we act *A Midsummer Night's Dream*," calls Miss Emmy, "so I hope you know your parts backwards by now!"

Us children are all dressed up in the costumes we're going to wear for the play. Standing about in the big garden of Cuttle Hall, we turn and look at each other with many an "oh!" and an "ah!" and shake our heads.

*"Coming a beard have I,"* shrieks Anthony Bone, giggling and leaping about on a pile of grass cuttings, *"Woman a play not me let, faith, nay!"* The show-off wants us to see he knows his lines off backwards.

Miss Emmy throws a black look in his direction, but Anthony doesn't care. He's used to those.

"What if a famous T.V. man came and grabbed one of us to be a television star!" cries Mary-Anne. We all know who she thinks the telly man would choose.

"He ought to spot *you* pretty quickly," says Arnie, "he'd probably want you for a game reserve."

She pouts, and puts her tongue out at him, then gathering up her long green skirt she runs over to the other girls. They have all donned pretty dresses now, and prance about to show themselves at their daintiest.

"We'll run through the dancing first," says Miss Emmy. "And you boys, behave yourselves, mind. If you dare damage the garden, you'll have Mr. Clarke on your tracks."

As we scatter in and out of the trees, I gaze unhappily up at the Big House. Here in this leafy garden I am not far from those very windows through which I saw Mam'selle.

"What's up, man?" Rodney asks. "You look fed up."

Rod had fastened on his beard and spectacles, and somehow these make him look old and wise. He looks like someone's great-grandfather.

"Can you keep secrets, Rod?"

"Try me!" He tosses head and looks at me firmly. Next thing is I start, in little chattering rushes, to unfold my tale.

Rodney listens carefully, moving grass with the toe of one shoe. He never interrupts, nor tells people what they already know, like many do.

"I tell you, Rod, it was like something on telly! Only this time I couldn't say to myself 'No need to get upset, it's only the telly,' because there she really *was*."

In my excitement I start tugging leaves off a low-hanging branch, and Rod pulls my hand away: "Steady on, you'll have old Crusty the gardener after you. Now listen." He looks me in the face. "I believe your Mam'selle Thingummy is a spy."

"A spy!"

"That's right."

"But we aren't at war with France!"

"How do you know she's French?"

"She speaks French, and she sings little French songs. Besides Captain Jenkins wouldn't bring a spy over."

"He may be a spy himself."

"Oh Rod, how can you?"

"That's what people always say, when other people turn out to be spies. Do you think spies go jumping about shouting 'I'm a spy, I'm a spy'? Why, they have to be mysterious, spies do."

"Yes, but what about Mr. Bob?"

"He may be the ringleader of the whole network."

"But if they're *all* spies—then why was he torturing Mam'selle?"

"Listen," says Rodney, who has answers for everything. "Maybe Mr. Bob isn't the real Mr. Bob at all. After all, when Captain Jenkins sent for him, he probably hadn't seen him for years and years. What if the *real* Mr. Bob got thrown overboard on the journey, and a pretend one took his place?"

"But I can't believe—"

"You say he stood there watching Mam'selle being bound and gagged! Well then, he's probably the ringleader of some foreign power. He's just posing as an English gentleman. Probably he was having Mam'selle tortured to extract secrets! And that other chap—"

"Sammy?"

"Yes, Sammy. Well, he's probably another one from Mr. Bob's gang. You say he acted very oddly at the fair. Well, then, most likely he captured your Mam'selle at the fair. Those were his orders."

"But Mr. Bob could have captured her in Ditchlington any day!"

"What, with all the nosey-parkers in the village watching him?"

"But how did he know she'd be at the fair?"

"I'll bet he knew her every move. I'll bet he was watching you getting on board that bus. If you're a Master Spy, you don't just *guess* what people are doing." Rodney nods his whiskery head gravely. "You *know*."

"What about Mrs. Odger, then?"

"Time will tell whether or not she's in the deadly gang."

Rodney's ideas are so clever that I begin believing him. "To think of Mr. Bob watching us, though! I bet every time we came out of the house, he saw us! And every time we went in, too! I saw a lot of creepy-looking people at the fair. Perhaps some of them were members of his gang."

One thing Rodney insists on; we must rescue Mam'selle at any price. Even if it costs us our lives.

He says this quite coolly, but I begin to shiver. A funny feeling comes into my stomach. Our lives! Then I remember how my Dad said once that very good people could live and die without other people even realising how good they were. I say to Rod, "Well, if it costs us our lives, let's hope people know about it. Let's hope they put pictures of us in the papers, and write about us and things."

I'm still looking at the Big House, so close to us, and so large. Suddenly it looks to me a dangerous place. I almost wish—well, not quite, but I wish—

"I daresay if they were to dump us in the canal, we'd be found eventually," Rodney remarks, "our bodies. I mean. They often drain canals."

*"Our bodies?"*

*"Are we all met?"*

"Did you say our bodies, Rod?"

*"Are we all met?"*

"I mean, Rod, perhaps if we were—"

"ARE WE ALL MET?"

It is Miss Emmy, yelling at Rodney, who has quite forgotten his part in the play. Hastily he shuffles forward across the grass, and unwinding the scroll, commences to play his part.

I keep my eye on the actors now, for soon it will be my turn to come in: *"And so everyone according to his cue"*; those are the words I have to say. The old men—Quince, Bottom, Snug, Snout and Starveling—are rehearsing their play, the one they plan to perform in front of the Duke and Duchess of Athens on their wedding night—Puck, of course, is a fairy, and in his eyes they are trespassing by being in the woods at all.

*"What hempen homespun have we swaggering here*
*So near the cradle of the fairy queen?"*

That's what I have to say.

Although a fine thing, and full of comic ways, our play used to seem to me just a strange story of happenings long ago. But now I feel less certain. Is a fairy lady going and falling in love with a donkey much stranger than Auntie Bette going all soft about Cyril? Is it not just as mysterious, too, that a French lady should vanish into a tent full of snakes and other creeping things, and later be glimpsed one night sobbing in a chair while a little man ties her up in knots?

"We're waiting for you, Puck!" Miss Emmy is waving at me, now; like Rodney I've gone and missed my cue. So giving the wreath of leaves on my head a bit of a tug (it's apt to slip) I run forward across the grass.

# *Chapter 11*

"HERE YOU are, Rod! I'm so glad to see you!"

I've been waiting for my friend up at the recreation ground. Now he draws into sight, a pencil and paper in his hand. He always believes in setting things down in black and white. We sink down on to the grass, and I select a piece to chew, while Rodney draws a picture of a mosquito.

"You do believe what I told you, don't you, Rod?"

Rodney is wearing a kind of cap to keep the sun out of his eyes, as they are rather weak. He looks at me coldly from under its peak. "Who said I didn't?"

"I just like being sure."

It seems that what Rodney is drawing is not a mosquito, it's the butterfly I saw up at the Big House. He's thorough, Rod is. "Now George, did you see any other strange characters lurking round that night?"

"I heard Henry yelling. And Mrs. Robb. Maybe someone on a bike."

"No cars mysteriously parked?"

"No. Look, here's Henry himself. Ask him, he was about that evening."

For who should come whizzing past on his blue bike, his legs stuck out like paddles, but Henry. The bike makes clanking noises, the spokes get caught in some long grass, and over goes the rider. Rodney rolls about on the ground laughing and Henry jumps on the bike and rides at Rod as hard as he can—but the grass stops him, and he's off again. Henry and Rod have a tussle, and Rod chases him across the fields. I climb on to the swing and go gently backwards and forwards, thinking to myself that it would be better not to question Henry, he's not a chap to trust.

Rod joins me, and we sit side by side, slowly rocking to and fro. "Somehow or other," Rod decides, "we've got to get into the cellar. That's the place they've chosen for her, likely."

"The cellar!"

"What's that story you told me once? The one Captain

Jenkins told you and Arnie? Something about smugglers."

"Wait a minute!" I look over the fields which are so far away that they seem flat and blue as the sea; and as my eyes search the big distance, I search my mind for this odd yarn.

"It was about some of his ancestors," I say slowly. "One in particular. He was a bit shady, the Captain said. He used to receive smuggled goods. You know, things like tobacco which nobody wanted to pay duty on. It seemed as though this chap went away once, and while he was gone somebody came with a warrant to search his house. The wife and the servants were scared, you see, because they didn't want him to get into trouble. They knew all the smuggled stuff was hidden down in the cellar.

"So they let in these policemen or whatever they were, and just as they were inside, the wife played a trick. She'd told her servants to load her horse with dummy packages, sort of suspicious-looking ones I suppose. Then she leapt on to her horse with a loud cry, sort of as if she was going to ride away taking the goods with her.

"At once the men turned round, and came after her. While they were gone, the wily servants took the stuff, the *real* stuff I mean, away from the house. Captain Jenkins said the poor wife rode so hard and so fast that the fright killed her; or the journey did. Her husband was so full of guilty sorrow that he became a monk."

"How interesting! I like that sort of story," says my friend. "Who knows, perhaps her ghost haunts the place to this very day?"

As I am not keen on ghosts I don't take him up on this. We sit swaying to and fro on the swings under the leafy branches.

"I know Mrs. Odger. She plays whist with my Mum," Rodney says. "She's ever so nice. Maybe if we were to tell her we are doing some psychical research, she'd let us investigate."

"Some *what*?"

"Sort of trying to find out about olden days, and what went on in old houses. There are societies that do that. They go all over your house with torches and things. They even bring blankets, and stay the night, if they think a ghost prowls in the early hours."

"Coo, sooner them than me!"

"We could say we were interested in that smuggling legend, if you're scared of ghosts then, George. Go on, we could make up something that would give us a chance to look in the cellar!" He seems quite excited, Rodney does.

But I'm still doubtful, and Rodney has to paint a colourful picture of Mam'selle suffering cruelly at the hands of her tormentors before I really wake up.

"Besides," says he, "it's you that used to be so fond of her. I hardly know her at all."

When he talks like that I take a big swallow and try to fall in with his plans.

# *Chapter 12*

MRS. ODGER listens kindly when Rod tells her what we want to do. People often listen carefully to Rod where they'd brush another child aside. He looks so serious.

"You see, Auntie Win, people who get interested in ghosts and stuff have to find out facts. They don't just want people saying 'Airy Tosh'."

"Airy tosh!" Mrs. Odger blows neatly into her tea cup to cool down the hot cupful she's just made. "Well, Rodney, I daresay I could let you hop down into the cellar for a moment, though what facts you'd find about a ghost, I can't imagine! Ghosts don't leave footsteps you know. Not like yours and mine, ghosts' feet."

I glance first at Rod's feet, then at Mrs. Odger's. Hers look too large for her brown shoes. She is a nice person, and not at all my idea of a spy.

Rod has his pencil out, and his book, and jots down a few notes. Mrs. Odger watches, her head on one side. "Sure it's not the police force you're training for, Rodney?"

"Just sharpening my powers of observation," says he.

"Well, well! Don't leave any shavings behind!" This sets her off doing a lot of chuckling, and the chuckling makes her pant. At last she fetches us both a biscuit from a pretty tin and suggests we go down into the depths right away.

"Best leave the cellar door open," she says, "in case the ghosts are extra nippy!" She opens the heavy-looking door, and we proceed down steep stone steps. And if there's one person who is wishing no one had ever mentioned ghosts, it's me.

I go first, and Rod follows, his pale torch lighting our

slow footsteps. For the rest, all is blackness.

Why, the cellar is bigger and loftier than I'd ever dreamed! The stone stairs behind us, Rod's torch drifts round far off stone walls; both of us stand staring. I can hear Rod's breathing, mine too, but nothing else. There are bottles everywhere. They're set out in rows in great tall racks, and maybe it's them that give the place its musty fruity smell. Suddenly Rod seizes me and pulls me over to a wall, and in a round spot of light his torch shows us these words scribbled there: "HURL YOUR THUNDERBOLT EVEN UNTO DEATH".

He nods big nods, as if to say "a clue!" Still we don't talk and by now I've found out a strange thing (though one perhaps well known to bats). It's this. When you're down in the dark, you don't dare to talk. All you do is make funny faces.

It's Rod who's making faces now. "Go on, go on!" his mouth moves round the words without speaking them: "Sing!" he commands, and with his hand he starts to pull imaginary notes out of his mouth.

Sing, indeed! The trouble is, this singing was *my* idea. I told Rod that if I was to sing Mam'selle's little French song down in the cellar, then our good friend might hear her rescuers.

I gulp. My lips are dry and I don't believe my throat is up to it. But Rod waves his arms hard, finally I open my mouth and utter a sort of croak:

*"Il etait une bergère*
*Et ron, ron ron, ron ron—"*

And then an answer comes.

At once my heart starts knocking so hard it's like a hammer. We clutch one another, Rod and I, and Rod gives my arm a dreadful squeeze. A brave boy, and nearer my own age than Arnie's, my poor friend like me is scared as mice.

"What a couple of cowards!" some might say. Ho! Well, let me ask you this: "Did *you* ever climb nearly alone down into a dark unknown cellar? Did *you* note it's all cold when you get down there, like a grave would be inside, and did you go there just after chattering about ghosts? Did *you* see tall steep steps and think what a lot of them it would seem if you were in a great hurry to get up them!"

"Aaaaaah—mmmmmmm—" the answer is a sort of groaning, stirring, waking noise, like a creature might make after being disturbed out of long years of sleep.

"Rod!" I whisper.

"Georgie!" he whispers back.

"Crikey!" cries my friend, and this word seems to act upon my spirits like a tall glass of beer. "Who's there?" I call out, clutching Rodney as hard as if he was my baby. "Who's there? Is that you, Mam'selle?"

"What? What? What?"

*"Oh,"* says Rodney. But his voice isn't scared any more. It's the exclamation of a chap who's come to his senses. "Oh, Captain Jenkins, Captain Jenkins!"

"What? Mm? What? Put a light on, can't you?"

"Where is it?" I ask, and the Captain's angry voice guides me to it. Click! The huge stone chamber is flooded with light. Our fanciful dreams flee like the shadows themselves and we stare round like owls blinking.

"Why didn't you tell us about that light?"

Mrs. Odger is making pastry. Rod leans over her large shoulder and whispers in her ear again. "You should have told us, Auntie Win!"

"Didn't want to spoil your fun, Rod," says she, at which my poor friend draws back bitterly, and no wonder. Fun, indeed!

But we boys are keeping quiet. The Captain is in a black mood. He sits glaring at the floor while Mrs. Odger does her best to coax him into a sweeter frame of mind.

"If only I'd known you were there, sir!" she cries, her big arms buried as far as the wrists in flour. "Why, I'd never have dreamed of letting the lads traipse down like that!" Her head goes on one side, her powdery hands go out.

"Pah!" says he. "I may not be the owner of Cuttle Hall, but as for the good wine laid down by my father in that cellar, why as you know, that wine is *mine*. There's no need for me to have to beg leave of the factotum before helping myself. Besides if I chose to take forty winks in the cellar (and mind I'm not ready to believe I did) it's as good a place as any."

I wonder what a factotum is. I glance at the Captain, who still looks sleepy in spite of his bad temper. Suddenly I'm reminded of our Dad. If we tell our Dad he went and dropped off in front of the telly, even if he's just come awake with a good snort, he always pretends he never went to sleep at all. "What's been happening, then, Dad?" we ask, just to tease him. And although he doesn't know, he'll never admit to taking a snooze.

"Look at that, too," says the Captain, showing a big rip in the sleeve of his jacket; "Tore it on a nail."

"But fancy your not putting on a light sir!" says Mrs. Odger and the Captain who has already explained this matter once, grabs a bottle of his precious wine in each hand, lifts both high, and throws up his eyes to the ceiling. When will she understand, he says testily, that there is more than one switch down there?

"A bulb went," says he.

"Jolly dark, wasn't it?" I say with a sigh. Suddenly the Captain unbends and starts to laugh. "Two pale faces," he says. "Two lads have had a fright. Well, I've given you my story—let's hear yours!"

I was afraid this question would arise, but just as I am clearing my throat to reply, Mrs. Odger tells him that we are writing a ghost story, and wanted to go down into the cellar to see what a cellar looked like. It's just as well she gives him this simple explanation, for I didn't want to tell a lie. The Captain is one of the best, but how could I tell him our weird fears about Mam'selle? Besides, he would only think we were off our rockers.

"Ghosts!" The Captain's loud laugh comes as a relief to all. "Where do you two chumps get your ideas from? You know what, my dear," he says to Mrs. Odger as she rolls out a blanket of pastry, "It's my belief they must learn mystery at school, not history." And then he asks us if ever we heard about the schoolboy who hissed a mystery lesson, tasted a whole worm, and was told to leave by the town drain?

Rod and I say no, we didn't.

"That's what they call a 'Spoonerism'," says the Captain, "there being once a certain absent-minded person called Mr. Spooner who used to get his letters in the wrong order. What he meant, you see, was that the boy missed a history lesson, wasted a whole term, and was told to leave by the down train."

Now Mrs. Odger fetches her work basket and neatly repairs the Captain's sleeve. What a relief it is to be back in the kitchen, to watch her needle flying to and fro in the Captain's jacket, to hear Tanjy purring! How bright and friendly the big room looks with its old scrubbed table, the big slow clock ticking on the wall, and pots of bright flowers on the sills!

Tanjy stretches himself out like cardboard and does a flying leap into the middle of the Captain's lap. The Captain fusses the old cat and spins a tale or two until the mending's done.

"So now my fine fellows, it's gone six, and your mothers will be waiting for such remains as the ghosts have let off lightly. I shall come with you, and each of you shall carry a bottle of my fine claret—but firmly, mind!"

As he reaches his cottage, the Captain's many dogs start barking and one or two try to get out. His waving arm signals goodbye, then the door is firmly banged.

For some time Rod and I walk along in silence. Then "Gosh!" I say.

"M," says my friend, patting his pocket, most likely to make sure his torch and note-book are inside.

"She wasn't down there, not in the cellar. Mam'selle, I mean. We know that now. And Rod," I add, "you don't *still* think Captain Jenkins is mixed up with some foreign plot, do you?"

"No. But it was odd, that light business."

"The bulb had gone."

"That's what he said."

All of a sudden the church bells start ringing. Old Mr. Bone is at his practising. Do-ng! Do-ng! Do-ng! Whenever I hear that noise I get a funny feeling. It's rather like this. It's as if each time a note struck, a massive cannon ball went rolling very straight, followed by another, then another, all sliding away into the distance and none of them disappearing. Just going rolling away somewhere else, then swelling up until all the air got full of them: do-ng, do-ng, do-ng.

"Do you *like* those bells, Rod?"

"It's only Mr. Bone."

"I'm glad we're out of that cellar."

"That's a good bit: *'Hurl your thunderbolt even unto death.'* Somebody must have written that years ago. I wonder who."

"Let's have it as a motto!"

"Were you scared down there?" asks Rodney, turning round his pale face.

"Cor, I was wondering whatever—"

"My teeth started chattering when I heard that noise!"

"That noise! When I heard it first!"

"Giving us such a fright. I wonder if we gave *him* a fright too? Perhaps that was why he got cross."

"He's been in the navy, and stuff. He'd be brave."

"You saying I'm a coward?" Rodney picks up a bit of a branch which must have fallen out of the heavy green trees that lean over the road and chucks it at me; I throw it back, and he finds another. *"Hurl your thunderbolt unto death!"* we shout. We find another branch, and another, and soon our running footsteps startle the old white horse and bring him charging across his field. Dodging each other's sticks and shouting we don't pass another soul until we reach our road. Then there's old Anthony Bone, lolling against his gate, seated on his bike and munching apples.

"Where've *you* been?" he calls out.

"Don't your wheels go round?" my friend retorts, then waving goodbye, he vanishes indoors for his tea.

"Where've you been?" Anthony asks again.

His pockets are bulging, like they always are after he's visited his Gran's. It must be nice to have such a generous Gran as Anthony's living close. On the other hand she does keep staring into the playground, looking for him. Just as well our Gran's up in the North! One should be thankful for small mercies, really.

# *Chapter 13*

EVERY DAY the sun keeps shining. It's the best summer for years, people say. Mothers dawdle by the wicker gate that leads to the playground, reluctant to go indoors; babies in their prams wear sunbonnets, and as for old Mr. Reynolds, he's never out of the flowers in his garden. Who wants to do lessons?

By afternoon we're fanning ourselves, and in play time even the boys drape themselves against the walls like tired lettuces. Only Arnie and Tommy Jenner stick to football, pelting round the hard playground, beetroot-faced, just as if they had never heard of it being too hot.

"I like your shorts!" "I like your dress!" "I like your shirt!" When the girls aren't admiring one another or annoying us boys, they're sitting against the walls, their eyes fast shut.

Wasps come dancing into the schoolroom through the high opened windows, the girls scream and Mary Stokes waves her work book so hard, the pages all fall out. Over-balancing to miss a wasp, Henry Robb knocks over the ink.

"I love wasps!" shouts Anthony Bone. "Wasps perch on me!" He stands on his chair with his arms held out shouting "I'm a statue, look, I'm Nelson!"

"Why have you got two arms, then?"

"I'm him before that, I'm him before the battle!"

"A statue can't put its tongue out."

"It wasn't his arm Nelson lost, it was his eye, so!" shouts Mary-Anne.

Some of the boys start drawing Nelson.

Rodney says nobody would make a statue of Nelson *before* the battle, what would be the point? It was the battle which made him famous.

"I'll tell you what my Dad says," Tommy Jenner calls out. "He says people write little bits about themselves, nice bits, if they're famous they do. And directly they pop off these bits go into the papers. Obituaries, they're called."

"I'll write Anthony's bittery!" shouts Henry Robb. " 'Anthony Bone was a curly-haired fat-faced nit and one day he fell off his bike—' "

Suddenly there is a loud scream. Trust Mary-Anne to go and be the one who got stung. "Ooh! Ow! Ooh!" She jumps about and covers her face and squeezes out some tears. This brings in our Head, Miss Worple, who up till now has been out of the room. "Why, whatever's the matter, Mary-Anne?"

Anthony has leaped off his desk and is muttering over his books again. "Who spilt that ink?" calls Miss Worple, and at last Henry is named. He goes off sulking to fetch a cloth. Miss Worple goes to look at Mary-Anne's sting and sends her to the First Aid cupboard for some ointment.

"Whatever is all this noise for? I've never heard such a noise in my life! Now all of you remember that there are only a few days left in which to learn your parts for the play. So take them home after school and learn them off by heart. And when I say off by heart," adds Miss Worple in her quiet majestic voice, "I mean *off by heart*."

"How can I keep learning roaring?" says Arnie as we head for home.

It's good to have our Mum about again, and find a cup of tea waiting back at home. Her cheeks are bright, she's singing, and she begs us boys to tell her tales about Auntie Bette and Mam'selle. "That French lady cooked a treat," Arnie tells her through a mouthful of bread and jam.

"What did she cook?"

"Better stuff than that Auntie-type person."

"What did she give you, though?"

"Oof! *She* gave us this awful raw cabbage."

"But the French lady, Arnie, what did she make?" our Mum says, and then our Will pops up from somewhere calling, "Cabbage, cabbage, little cabbage, that's what the

Mummy-lady called me."

"One gives you cabbage, and one *calls* you cabbage. I don't know," says our Mum pulling Willy on to her lap. "So where is she? Has anybody heard a thing about her? It's a long time now."

"Most likely she has gone back to France," says Arnie, "that's what they're all saying."

I put my knife and fork together and go into the garden. Having a secret such as mine is no happy matter. Knowing things other people don't may be fine if they are nice things. But if they are sorry facts, then what is there to feel proud about?

I sink down on to our back doorstep and open up my part in the play. It's lucky I can read my own writing, it's rather a scribble.

I know the stuff pretty well all except for the bits at the very end. Once the old men have acted their play in front of the Duke of Athens and his bride, and the duke, stepping forward has said:

> *"The iron tongue of midnight hath told twelve*
> *Lovers to bed, 'tis almost fairy time—"*

Then it's for Tommy Jenner (in his part of Oberon king of the fairies) and I (in my part of special fairy attendant) to bring the whole thing to a close.

> *"Now the hungry lion roars*
> *And the wolf behowls the moon*
> *Whilst the heavy ploughman snores—"*

I shut my eyes and try to repeat the lines. I think to myself that if I was really a spirit, I could magic the whole lot into my head. As well as that, if I forgot on the great

LA SAINTE UNION
COLLEGE OF EDUCATION
THE AVENUE, SOUTHAMPTON

day I could render myself invisible—click! Where's Puck? *"Now the angry lion roars—"*

No! *"Now the hungry lion roars—"*

"I'll get you, Henry my lad!" It's Mrs. Robb's shrill bellow: she's chasing Henry round the garden. He's knocked a big flower pot over, and he's kicking it about. I decide it would suit Henry to be a spirit. He'd like that better than being a boy. He's too mischievous as it is. But the tricks he could play if he was a spirit!

Mrs. Robb is out there beating a carpet—she always does her housework late. And there goes Miss White, creeping back from the shop with a carrier bag. Now if Henry was Puck, he could turn into that carpet, and then putting on Miss White's squeaky voice cry out "Why Mrs. Robb, whatever are you doing to me! Ooh Mrs. Robb, stop beating me at once indeed—" Then in my mind's eye I see the old carpet go whirling down the road, and Mrs. Robb running after it: "Come back! Come back!" she's shouting. Then all of a sudden flop—stop—it's curled itself round and fallen flat into the middle of the road; over it goes Anthony Bone on his bicycle. And as for Henry, why he's back in his own garden leaning over the hedge and calling out "Why, Mum, what's our carpet doing in the middle of the street?"

Shaking these fancies away I go back to learning my lines.

*"And we fairies that do run*
*By the triple Hecate's team*
*From the presence of the sun*
*Following darkness like a dream—"*

Following darkness. These words take me back to the

cellar. I think about Rod and I blundering about down there, and I wonder if Captain Jenkins told Miss Emmy about it?

But after all, Mam'selle *was* there up at the Big House—where is she now? If she's kept in some other secret place, then Mrs. Odger must surely know about it. You couldn't keep things like that a secret from her. But Mrs. Odger couldn't be a villainess could she, what, and her so chuckly and kind and free with the biscuits?

*"And we fairies that do run*
*Following darkness like a—"*

I have a new vision now. It's a vision of a bottle of milk and the secret of this bottle of milk is this. It isn't a bottle of milk at all. It's really Puck. He's magicked himself into it. He sits outside the Big House early in the morning, then gets picked up and taken inside.

But he doesn't stay as that milk bottle. Oh no. Next thing he's a mouse. And now he's darting from room to room, scattering powdery plaster and wood as he scrapes away with his magic fingers, and going into every single room in that place in search of missing Mam'selle.

How about Tanjy, though?

Could a cat eat a spirit?

Shutting my eyes very tightly I try and imagine Tanjy as twenty times my size. I see his whiskers big as ropes, his bright eyes the size of car-lamps, and his big orange furry head and body the size of a whole room.

Poor mice! What they have to put up with, when you think of it.

# Chapter 14

ALL AT once it's Friday, the day of the play.

There's a lovely sky it's full of clouds but only large white ones, with a small wind to keep them high up in the sky. All of us are thankful, for who wants to sit outside and watch a play from under a mac?

We always get good dinners at the end of term. Today it's hot mutton with red currant jelly, and a pretty, pudding-looking birthday cake. But I'm too excited to eat a lot. *"Methinks I have a great desire for a bottle of hay!"* Henry calls, and directly we reach the garden up at Cuttle Hall, he finds a pile of grass cuttings and starts munching them.

"Tie my head on, Georgie, put on my head," he begs, so once again I fit the old donkey head over his own. As usual, it slips down too far over his nose.

Miss Emmy has arranged for music to come from the house, to make all gay. A few mothers have started straggling across the lawn, and soon our Mum is waving to me among them. Dressed in their fairy clothes the girls hand out the programmes—these have paintings on, and inside our names are written. I've seen mine.

"Puck - - - - George Burtwood," it says.

Mary-Anne twists a bow in her blue shimmering dress, and bumps into Henry.

"Do you believe in fairies, George?" he asks, adding,

"I *used* to when I was a little chap, but then I saw a big elephant today, and it put me off."

Mary-Anne scolds him. He turns a somersault, and off flies the donkey's head.

"Sh!" calls out Miss Worple. Miss Emmy throws a warning look at us—for by now we should be gathered in our places in the grove of trees, and ready, from behind bushes, to come on each in turn.

It's Rod who has to go in first. I bet his teeth are chattering. It's all very well for show-offs like Mary-Anne, but my friend is more sensitive. Luckily he has his scroll; he thought he'd lost it at dinner time. Seeing him in his wire spectacles and little beard, and hearing his speeches I start

forgetting he's Rodney my friend, and imagining he really is a strange old carpenter called Quince.

It's the same with all of us. I forget we're boys and girls, what with our wearing beards and cloaks, and the girls such pretty dresses.

*"Here is a scroll of every man's name which is thought fit, through all Athens, to play in our interlude before the Duke and Duchess on his wedding day at night!"* announces Quince.

*"First, good Peter Quince, say what the play treats on; then read the names of the actors, and so grow to a point!"* Bottom insists, dancing about with impatience. But when

he hears the names of the characters, he wants to be them all.

*"Let me play Thisbe too,"* he begs, *"I'll speak in a monstrous little voice: 'Thisne, Thisne; Ah Pyramus, my lover dear—'"*

Suddenly among all the laughter I hear one special laugh which stops me still. But I daren't look out, I daren't show myself from inside the bushes. And even when I prance on and get talking with a fairy, and she says she knows all about Puck, and reels off some of his naughtiest tricks, still I don't dare try and trace the source of that laughter. "Never look into the audience," Miss Emmy has warned us, "you might catch somebody's eye, and break the spell."

Here comes Oberon, quarrelling with his fairy queen. He looks the picture of a king. I made his crown myself, those are real beads stuck on the cardboard with glue. Now he is asking me to fetch him the dangerous little flower. Holding it in his hand, he tells of his plan to bewitch Titania:

*"I know a bank where the wild thyme blows*
*Where ox-lips and the nodding violet grows*
*There sleeps Titania some time of the night*
*Lulled in these flowers with dances and delight—"*

Back in the bushes, I catch hold of my brother's sleeve.

"Arnie!"

"Sh."

*"Arnie!"*

Now the fairies are dancing, and all have a song to sing. They twist and caper round their sleeping queen, putting a spell upon her, driving away snakes, black beetles, worms and snails.

"Arnie, *look*—" I whisper.

My brother makes warning, rabbity faces. I pull on his sleeve and make such faces back that he feels bound to obey. "What?" he wants to know, and pointing through the leaves I say "There—look!"

"Whew!" It's a sort of silent whistle my brother makes as his breath goes in sharply. His eyes grow bigger and bigger and his round face lights up like morning sunshine. He turns to me all smiling.

"What?" Rodney whispers, moving nearer as he sees our excitement. But there's no time to speak to him, for the play's the thing. In no time we've to tumble on again, first Puck with the donkey's head, then Arnie with his lion's costume on, then Quince with his list of directions.

When the old men come to acting their play in front of the Duke and Duchess, the audience are in fits of laughter. There's Bottom all dressed up in aluminium tinfoil, and "Wall" wearing a costume made of paper painted to look like bricks.

"*Show me thy chink, to blink through with mine eye!*" cries Pyramus. Then "Wall" holds up his thumb and finger to make this chink. On strides Thisbe, played by the old man called Francis Flute. He wears a long dress and a yellow wig and cries squeakily

*"Oh Wall, full often hast thou heard my moans*
*My cherry lips have often kissed thy stones!"*

The two lovers Pyramus and Thisbe agree to meet at a place called Ninny's Tomb. But just as Thisbe gets there,

Lion arrives and roars so fiercely that poor old Thisbe dashes off in a fright. She leaves her cloak behind, and Lion savages it, still roaring. Arnie never roared better in his life.

When Pyramus finds the cloak all bloodstained, for Lion has just finished some raw dinner, he thinks his loved one is dead. Sadly he plunges his sword into his chest. *"Now I am dead, now I am fled, die, die, die!"* he moans, sinking into the grass.

A moment later back creeps poor Thisbe, *"What, dead my dove? These lily lips, this cherry nose, these yellow cowslip cheeks?"* with a scream she sticks his sword into her own heart and falls down dead on top of him.

And so our play is done.

Music floats on to the summer air. It's ever such pretty music, though a bit weird too. The boys bow low, the girls curtsey, and a whole lot of clapping takes place.

The sun shone down, the rain kept off, I never forgot a single line of my part. But best of all—here *she* is! Not sad and bowed like last time I saw her, but clapping like mad, with beaming face—yes, it's our long lost Mam'selle!

"Georgie! Arnold!" As we run across the grass to meet her she stoops down to hug us and pat our cheeks.

"Where have you been?" Arnie wants to know.

"Ah, the story is too long for me to tell you now, but soon you shall hear it!" As Henry Robb dashes past she catches hold of him. "This little boy—he is a donkey—we are the same, he and I. And what is it you say, Donkey?"

Henry is always glad to do some talking by request. "I know!" he shouts, dancing about. Then he stops for a moment and puts his hands behind his back:

*"I have had a dream. Man is but an ass if he can go about to expound this dream. Man is but a patched fool if he will offer to say what methought I had. The eye of man hath not heard the ear of man hath not seen, man's hand is not able to taste, his tongue to conceive nor his heart to report what my dream was—"*

"Ah!" cries she. "The eye hath not heard, the ear does not see, the tongue can hardly tell this dream! *My* story, it is not a dream—but ah, what a bad dream! But see, I am awake; pinch me. So! Now, go to your nice tea, your cakes and bonbons. Your teacher, she is waving."

"Just tell me this, Mam'selle," I plead, fingering the bow on her pink belt, "were you ever up at the Big House, in that room there?" and I point towards Cuttle Hall. But Miss Worple is shouting to us to join the other children who are sitting together on mats on the ground.

"Yes, yes," Mam'selle nods busily. "But I speak to your mother, yes? I come to your house, Georgie. Go now, go—" then she calls after us "Very nice, your play it is! This lion roaring—ah!" And she throws up her eyes and pretends to run from Arnie.

So we run over to claim our tea. Arnie roaring and Henry Robb yelling out "Bags the most, bags the most, bags the most!"

Rod beckons me to a place beside him. "Did she tell you all about what happened?" he asks. It seems the gossips have already been giving Mam'selle's story a strong flavour. "Is it true," he asks me, "that Mam'selle was gored by a tiger?"

"Whoever said *that*?" I want to know. Rod tells me it was Mary-Anne.

As we sit round in a circle lemonade starts coming

round, big jugfuls of it. There are sandwiches coming too, and red buns. Little Willy sits cross-legged among the infants gazing at the spread with loving eyes.

"I can't wait to hear Mam'selle's story," I say to Rod. "She looks pretty well and blooming to me."

"Not like she'd been in a cellar—" this idea tickles both of us, and we start laughing. Our Will joins in. He always joins in laughter, even when he doesn't know the joke.

Here's Miss Emmy coming round with the biscuits. Everybody wants to speak to her. "Was I all right, Miss Emmy?" "Could you hear me?" "Was my dancing nice?" "I forgot that bit about the mouse!"

Kindly she smiles down at us and says yes, everything went so well, she is very proud of us all. But suddenly she turns round with even more of a smile; Mr. Bob has come over to talk to her. Seeing him put his hand on hers, I think that perhaps Mam'selle's prayers will come true; perhaps they'll marry, and both live together up at Cuttle Hall.

"The play was excellent, excellent," he says, "did I recognise my dining room curtains on King Oberon's shoulders?" I've never seen him in such a good humour. Mrs. Odger, all dressed up in her best, hands him a bottle of orangeade to undo. The top's ever so tightly fixed. Suddenly bang! It's unfixed, and some spills on the velvety lawn. All laugh, nobody seems cross today.

Why should they be? What is there to be cross about?

Across the lawn I hear a burst of laughter from Mam'selle. With a sigh I tell myself that whatever bad times she's been through, they are over now. The deadly Juice didn't do its worst. Here she is, jolly as ever, back in our midst once more.

# Chapter 15

MAM'SELLE ARRIVES at our house that very evening.

"Ah, how I feel at home! This is the place I shall always call my home in England!" She throws out her hands to us two big boys and to little Willy, who is sitting on the floor clutching his rabbit and gazing up at her. "These good boys," she tells our Mum and Dad, "you see how they have been good to me! I came to their house to look after them and then it is they, not they, but I, who does this stupid thing."

Her ear-rings flash, that pink dress is surely her best get-up. She sits there beaming at us.

"As long as it wasn't *them* who were behind the trouble," our Dad says good-humouredly.

"Why, how *can* you, Dad?" asks Arnie, all big-eyed.

"Oh, please do tell us all!" I beg her, but our Mum says kindly that Mam'selle must begin just when she wants. Why, she must be tired after all her adventures.

"We want to know," says Arnie simply.

"A cup of tea? A cup of coffee?" asks Dad, springing up. He is hospitality itself this evening.

"Ah, the coffee, yes, thank you. It is true that I have had some adventures very strange. Soon you will see, my boys, why I say to your friend the donkey 'I too have had a dream'. But do not be angry with me! For now you see I am safe again and sound."

*"Safe and sound, safe and sound, wind of the Western Sea,"* sings our Willy, sucking his thumbs and leaning back against Mam'selle.

She pats his head, tells him that he is one of Heaven's angels, and thanks our Dad for the cup of coffee he has brought her. "But you must bear with me, my dears, if I have this bad English. Since we were together, I have not had by me my dictionary, and I make many mistakes. Ah, but the worst mistake, now you shall hear it!

"Is it not so long since we went happily to the fair? No, it is not so many days, but for me it is like a year. You remember how I wished so much to see this lady who lay in a glass box? Many people come like me to stare at this young girl so brave and beautiful who can lie in such a place with rats and snakes who crawl everywhere! But I see no door in this glass box. How did she get in there, I ask myself? About such little matters I am very curious. Then I see a little gold button. Ah! I put my hand on this thing! Is there a lock perhaps which must usually be fastened? Tonight it is not so. A snake small but hideous puts out his head.

"Ah, what pain! How I scream! Next I remember nothing, all is black. When I awake, I find myself in a very small room; I am lying on a bed. My poor arm! It is big like a hippopotamus. The pain it is so bad I cannot easily move. But where am I? Am I on a ship? For I see now that this little room it moves along. But wheels are turning underneath, and now I see all. This is a caravan, and your Mam'selle, she is travelling with the fair!

"An old woman is seated near to me. She is knitting, this old woman, and when she does not look at her stitches she is watching me. She sings, but it not like our pretty songs; it is more a noise, you understand, like when you rub a piece of wood.

"'Where are we?' I say to her, 'where are you taking me?' But all she will say, this cross old person, is that we will arrive no quicker when she tells me the name of the town.

"Now a man comes to see me. He has big whiskers, this man, and his face it is red. He is a big man, and strong. 'Madam,' shouts he, 'you did a very foolish thing. Very very foolish! It is lucky for you that you are not more hurt. Now we look after you, and you stay with us until your arm is better. If you try to escape, some bad thing will happen to you—you understand?' And he brings his face close and cross to mine.

"I look quickly for my handbag, for I think that I will surely disobey this man, but it is not near me! It has been hidden! I am indeed a prisoner.

"Drrum, drrum, the wheels are turning again! From a little window I see houses, trees, the sun. In the night only we are still; then perhaps a day after it seems we are stopped at some town. People are busy everywhere; there are shouts and much noise. I think this old woman, this Rose, for that is her name, she is pleased, for she puts away her knitting in a cupboard, and when a lady puts her head round the door this old Rose she shouts to me 'Stay there, mind!' Then she is gone.

"I listen to hear a key turn, but this is not so, and now with my arm hurting only a little I am able to rise up and creep to the door. Outside the air is dark and damp, for it is evening with a little rain. I move between caravans, of which there are many, keeping away from the strong lights. Then I see written on one of these a word, perhaps the angels have guided me to this word, for it is written 'Lawyer' and I know what it means, this word 'lawyer'. So I dare to knock on the door of this place.

"A little man opens it. 'Come in!' he says kindly, as if he knew me well, 'Come in my dear!' and he is smiling at me.

"What a nice little place I find, so warm and like a little palace! Quickly this little man fetches brandy, and he hands me his card, on which are written these words: 'Sammy Sawyer, your Friend through Thick and Thin.'

"As I tell my story to Mr. Sawyer, the tears start to run

down my cheeks, for I believe I have found a friend. Indeed, this little man knows of me; he knows of my experience with the snake and he reveals to me what he believes is this snake man's plan. It is to put me down in some strange town through which his caravan is travelling, so that I am not able to find him again and go perhaps to the police and give his name. These snakes, they are not poisonous but it is a bad thing for this man that a person like myself should so easily put out my hand and have a bite.

"I eat a little cake, because Mr. Sawyer wants much I eat his nice cake, but I not a good appetite. I am afraid that this old Rose, she comes to find me. But Mr. Sawyer, he says he is a match for this silly old woman, he will hide me, and he will find a way to take me back to my good friends. For I have told him now of Miss Emmy and Mr. Bob, and of my dear boys (and indeed, he knows you, yes? You have visited him that first night when I am lost my kind boys! This he tells me).

"Then he says we are not so very far from Ditchlington, after all, for the fair, it moves round and round to small towns, and if to me it seems we must have covered all of your country, indeed this is not so. But he goes quickly to speak to Mr. Bob upon the telephone, for he says that now I am free we must hurry away as fast as it is possible.

"Ah, how good is this little man! On the journey he will not let me be sad. We drive for many miles and he sings to me the funny songs and tells stories of his magic. Then he says to me 'Now do you know where we are? Do you think you know this place?' and certainly then I see this church, this white house on the corner—we have arrived at Ditchlington!

"Soon we are in the great house of Mr. Bob. Before I never knew how kind is this gentleman! Now I see he is a man of much good sense. A big meal is prepared, and Mr. Sawyer plays many tricks. I think he is like Puck, a little, George! He makes jokes, and he plays tricks with ropes, with cards, with money. He fetches from Mr. Bob's pocket pound notes; he makes jump a little frog. It is so funny, yes, but when I think of the trouble I am to these good friends, the tears, they flow!

"But the man with snakes, you will ask, how does he feel when he finds his prisoner gone? Does he, as you say, wallop this old Rose? Ah, this man, I do not see him again! For Mr. Bob, he has a plan. He goes to find the man and tell him I am safe, and that no more of this bad happening shall be said. The police shall never know—indeed, it is a little my fault of course, to play with the little golden handle. The snake surely makes no bite unless a person opens the glass case. And Mr. Bob, he is sure that for the future, the man will put on his box a very strong lock.

"But, you will say, why do you not come running to see us in our house at Ditchlington? Ah, my boys, I am still a little afraid! I seem to see the man with whiskers in angry mood searching for his lost lady! For a few days, I say to myself, I will rest in Cuttle Hall, I will stay safely in this large house. Then none shall see me, or pass on this message to another. But one thing I have decided, I must come to see your good play! I must see what happens to this other lady who has a strange adventure after her eyes are bathed in the juice of a little flower! I must see the gentleman who naughty Puck turns into a donkey! And so it is today I step out safely into the world again to tell my strange adventures!"

Arnie lets out a great sigh and his eyes goggle at Mam'selle in wonder. Willy has fallen asleep, with the ears of his big rabbit folded across his chest. Our Dad shakes his head and scratches it and beams, then goes out to the back to do something to his boots.

"What a time you've had," cries our Mum, "and to think it was the boys we told to take care!"

But there's something I want to know badly. "Mam'selle, if ever anybody offered you a bottle of that juice again, would you go near it in all your life?" I ask her.

"To risk having such adventures again? Never!" she cries, laughing as she pats my shoulder.

"Then you do really believe there might be something —well, *special* about that juice?"

"Of course!" She shrugs, smiling, as if there can be no doubt about such a matter.

"Pooh," says Arnie, "just some old juice out of a flower."

"Ah, but how many things there are round us that we do not understand *'The tongue can't see it, the ear cannot tell it—'* as your old donkey man says. But indeed, your Shakespeare, he is a giant, and he knew of many things we cannot ourselves understand."

Our Mum asks Mam'selle if old Rose fed her properly. Mam'selle says she was given mostly cups of tea and chips. "How many cups of tea! And always this kettle steaming! So bad for the chest. But I find one book to read, and this for me is good. I speak so badly your English, but to read I am better, you understand. And in this book are such adventures! Fires, and lions, and fightings, and so much that is brave! I did not know it well, this

Bible, but now in my bad days I read gladly of many others who have suffered and come in the end to a better time."

"I like books that are funny," says Arnie.

"Ah yes, for that which thinks itself too important for laughing, bang, down it goes! But here too are funny stories—what about the wife of this David who makes instead a dummy in his bed, so that when the king's men come to stab him, he is far out in the forest? You like this story?"

"You ought to have made a dummy of yourself to put in your bed," Arnie says, "that old Rose person might never have noticed you'd run off."

"Did you ever get your handbag back?"

"Ah yes. Mr. Bob, he has fetched it for me. And to comfort them, he has whispered, too, to your father and mother that I am safe again. But to you, my dear boys, I like best to appear, as you say, out of the blue! To come back as suddenly as I vanished—plof!" she beams, and pats our heads. "And now here I am, in this kind house which put out to me always its arms. The place where I cook with the boys and we sing and make jokes until your good mother she is better. When I go, I carry always good memories of your family!" she tells our Mum.

"I bet you carry awful memories of that old Rose," I say. "What was *she* doing at a fair?"

"Ah Georgie, Arnie, this old Rose! Always her stupid eyes watching me. Sitting, knitting, peeping. And these chocolates of hers! Frequently she opens this box of chocolates to see little picture which shows her each different one. But to eat which, this she cannot decide! So again the box is closed. Ah, the rustling of this box, it gets on my nerves—until one day, boum! The caravan has stopped. Suddenly all are on the floor. And now she must throw all away, she says, except two which do not come out. And of these two, one is a nut. She has not good the teeth, so this nut she cannot eat."

"Why doesn't she give you the nut and eat the other?"

"Ah but then she has not this thing to do! To open the box, to rustle the paper, to make her plan to eat one day. You see how many there are who must hide their dreams, and take them out only to have a look. Then they will be put in a cupboard." Mam'selle nods in her knowing way.

"Like you put away your Shakespeare, Arnie, saying you're going to read a whole play of his next time," I say to Arnie.

"That's different, idiot," says Arnie, aiming a cushion at me.

"It's always different when it's you!" I'm laughing at him, so he picks up a cushion and buries my head in it. We start rolling together all over the sofa. But Dad soon puts a stop to this sort of thing, and half an hour later we find ourselves in bed.

"What goings on, Arnie!" Lying upstairs, I'm gazing at the ceiling, half watching a moth up there, my mind full of Mam'selle's strange story.

"I'll say. Fancy undoing that box. She ought to have known better."

"But the Juice—you do believe Arnie, that all that stuff had something to do with her putting the Juice on her lids?"

"Dunno."

"It must have done! Like they said, there are lots of

things people still don't know."

"I expect a real scientist could explain."

"Scientists! You're bad as Rod the way you crack them up. They're only ordinary people with brains that can take a lot in, and lots of money behind them. An old scientist know it all? Pooh! What, those great seas, seven of them, and great hills and high mountains with fossils and precious stones inside? How could anybody explain all those? What about dark forests at night, with funny noises, and hyenas barking, and elephants swishing their tails and their trunks in the banana groves?" I'm getting quite excited, I sit up in bed waving my arms about. "Beavers bringing trees down with their teeth, and crabs, and underground caves, and volcanoes and glaciers! Fire and seaweed and oysters and sudden earthquakes! Why the world being such a massive place, and all of us being so tiny compared to one tall tree even—who do we think we are, with brains the size of a little bunch of grapes?"

"That's your trouble, you like mysteries," says Arnie. "Why not become an explorer? Go and get animals for fairs and things." The moth comes near to him and he tries to swipe it.

"I might. But I think I'd rather just let them be. I mean it's bad luck to make a snake sit about in a glass cage when it could be chasing about in its natural habitat."

"My natural habitat," says Arnie, "is to be a millionaire and lie by a swimming pool giving orders."

"You natural habitat is—is—"

While I'm trying to think of a cheeky enough place, my brother says that he reckons Mam'selle's story would make a good book.

"That's what I'm going to do, man, write it down!" I

tell him eagerly.

"What, with *your* spelling?"

"A person can get that corrected."

"And your writing?"

"A person can get books typed out. A secretary does it."

My brother has started to chuckle. As usual he can't stop once he's started. He is rocking away in his bed, and I ask him what's up.

"I saw a picture," he explains, "this bird, see. A great big thing it was, nearly black. Sort of stringy-looking, like Auntie Bette—"

Arnie is laughing so much now that he has a job to speak. "It was called—it was called—a—a—Secretary Bird."

Laughter gets caught easily in our family. Soon I am joining him. "Was it—was it up a tree, Arnie?"

"On—on the ground. It would be too—too big for a tree." Laughing comes over him in fresh bursts. "Big and black—sitting there—with sort of things like pencils behind its ears—"

"Its *ears*?"

"Well—you know—and horrible eyes, it had."

But now comes a rap on the door. Our Dad is telling us to keep quiet. When his steps have died away I say to Arnie that I shall employ a Secretary Bird to do my typing. Arnie says the unions would shoot it. But he keeps giggling away to himself and saying over and over the title "Secretary Bird" which just seems to tickle his fancy.

Listening to him sets me off thinking once more about the odd creatures that inhabit our globe. About snakes, and hippos and iguanas. And about how it is that we humans rule the world, not they.

Or is it? What lies behind our lives, really? Behind the trees and the people and the mountains?

"Arnie," I say, "do you suppose—"

Suddenly our front door opens. I hear voices saying good night. Our Mum, Dad, Mam'selle. Probably they are hugging one another—Mam'selle often hugs people.

They do that a lot in France. There's our Dad at the gate shouting "No more snakes, remember! Don't go opening any more cages!" and from the doorway Mum is begging Mam'selle to keep in touch: "Send us a postcard from time to time."

A postcard from France! That would be good.

Now there's old Miss White's door opening—trust her to try and find out what's going on. She's got hold of Mrs. Robb, who's just home from Bingo most likely. "Good evening, Mrs. Robb. Hasn't it been a lovely day?"

"Oh, hasn't it? My Henry took the part of a donkey in the play. Ever so good, he was. Why, Henry, come back!"

But Henry's feet clatter down the road. He'll do anything rather than go to bed. That was a good trick Puck played on him, turning him into a donkey! The little flower worked wonders. Come to think of it, where did I last see that flower juice?

"Arnie!" I call again.

But I'm talking to deaf ears. My millionaire's asleep. He's never such a restless one as I. So after I've said my prayers and looked at the stars and shut the window to keep out any moths, I crash my head on the pillow, bring the sheet round my ears, and join Arnie in the land of dreams.

Until tomorrow.

Tomorrow, I'm going to start my story.

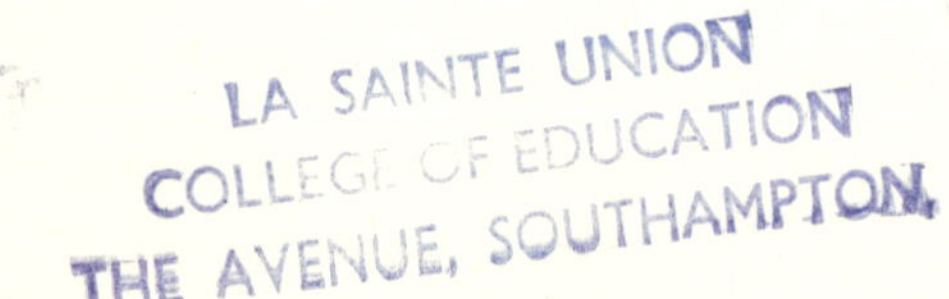